"Come....come with me," Roxanne whispered.

She turned and headed for the staircase, acutely aware of him behind her—her heart pounding as she led him into her room. Briefly she saw him glance around in surprise and she thought that the fairly featureless little bedroom must look so very different to his own, back in the great house.

Outside, their lives were so dissimilar, she thought. But in this anonymous little room, those differences didn't matter. He might be a duke and she might be a singer who'd fallen on hard times, but in this one very fundamental act, at least— they were equals.

"Is this better?" she questioned as she went into his waiting arms.

"Much. And this is better still." His mouth brushed over hers with a featherlight tease. "Don't you think?"

SCANDAL
IN THE SPOTLIGHT

The truth is more shocking than the headline!

Named and most definitely shamed, these media
darlings have learned the hard way that the press
always loves a scandal!

Having a devastatingly gorgeous man beside them
only adds fuel to the media frenzy. Especially when
the attraction between them burns hotter and brighter
than the paparazzi's flashbulbs…

If you missed
Michelle Conder's GIRL BEHIND THE
SCANDALOUS REPUATION
and
Caitlin Crews's HEIRESS BEHIND THE HEADLINES
both titles are available in ebook!

Sharon Kendrick

BACK IN THE HEADLINES

SCANDAL
IN THE SPOTLIGHT

HARLEQUIN®

entertain, enrich, inspire™

Recycling programs
for this product may
not exist in your area.

ISBN-13: 978-0-373-23871-2

BACK IN THE HEADLINES

www.Harlequin.com

Printed in U.S.A.

All about the author…
Sharon Kendrick

SHARON KENDRICK started storytelling at the age of eleven and has never really stopped. She likes to write fast-paced, feel-good romances with heroes who are so sexy they'll make your toes curl!

Born in west London, she now lives in the beautiful city of Winchester—where she can see the cathedral from her window (but only if she stands on tiptoe). She has two children, Celia and Patrick, and her passions include music, books, cooking and eating—and drifting off into wonderful daydreams while she works out new plots!

Visit Sharon at www.sharonkendrick.com.

Other titles by Sharon Kendrick available in eBook:

Harlequin Presents®

CHAPTER ONE

IT WAS the seediest nightclub he'd ever seen and Titus Alexander couldn't quite hide his instinctive shudder of distaste. Heedless of the curious glances his aristocratic good looks were attracting, he adjusted his powerful frame in the flimsy chair and looked around.

The place was half full of people you wouldn't want to bump into on a dark night and the waitresses wore costumes which might have been considered sexy if they hadn't all been carrying an extra thirty pounds. He froze to find an enormous pair of breasts wobbling perilously close to his face, as he was served a cocktail he was never going to touch. And not for the first time, he wondered who in their right mind would ever choose to work in a dive like this.

Leaning back in his seat, he stared at the stage and reminded himself that he wasn't here to critique his surroundings or to reflect that he'd never been in such a low-rent place before. He was here to see a woman. A woman who…

His thoughts were halted by the tinny fanfare of a piano and the slightly slurred voice of the compère who had been introducing a succession of failing acts all evening.

'Ladies and *Gentle*men! Tonight, I am proud to present a singing *legend*. A woman who has had number one hits in thirteen different countries. Who, with her girl-band The Lollipops, has known the kind of fame that most of us only ever dream of. She's consorted with royalty and politicians—but tonight she's exclusively ours. So I ask you to give it up for the beautiful and talented Miss…Roxanne…*Carmichael*!'

The applause in the half-empty club was sporadic and Titus mimed a brief clapping as he watched the woman appear from the wings, his body automatically tensing as she took centre stage.

Roxanne Carmichael.

His eyes narrowed. Was that really *her*?

He'd heard a lot about her. Read a lot about her. He'd seen her staring back at him from old magazine covers, with her cat-like eyes and a sleek body which had advertised everything from diamonds to raincoats. She stood for everything he despised, with her loud, flashy beauty and a long list of lovers which appalled him—because he had the sexual double standards of many of his class. He wasn't sure what he'd been expecting when he encountered her in the flesh for the first time—but it certainly wasn't this deep, tightening clench inside him, which felt uncomfortably like the beginning of lust. And he couldn't for the life of him work out why.

Maybe it was because she looked nothing like the provocative creature whose girl-band had stormed the international charts all those years ago. Back then, she'd sported deliberately ripped stockings worn with a too-short school uniform and was always seen sucking provocatively on a lollipop, which had helped give the band their name. As their success had grown the sticky lollipops had been jettisoned along with the jail-bait clothes—but the image projected to the public had still been that of sexy bad girls. The kind of woman you wouldn't want to take home to meet your mother. And Roxanne Carmichael had certainly lived up to her reputation as a wild child.

He let his gaze flicker over her body. The passing of the years hadn't added any extra weight to her frame. In fact, apart from the luscious curve of her breasts— were they *real*? he wondered—she looked almost painfully slender. Her cheekbones were emphasised by deep shadows beneath them and her jaw was sharply defined. Without the glossy exterior provided by extreme wealth, her mane of hair was no longer teased into a myriad shades from honey through to bronze, but now hung in a natural dark-blonde curtain over her shoulders.

But her eyes were still that incredible shade of blue and her lips still looked as if they were capable of inciting a man to commit sin. Despite the faded jeans and the sequined shirt, she carried herself with a natural grace, Titus conceded—but she looked tired. And jaded. Like a woman who had seen too much, too often. *I'll bet she has*, he thought grimly as she picked up the microphone and held it close to her scarlet lips.

'Hi, everyone.' Her lashes fluttered as her gaze darted around the room. 'My name is Roxy Carmichael and tonight I'm here to entertain you.'

'You can entertain me any time you like, Roxy!' yelled an unsteady male voice from the back of the dark club and somebody laughed.

There was a pause—Titus thought she looked as if she was about to change her mind. For one brief moment, she looked almost *vulnerable*. As if someone had got her up on stage by mistake and she was unsure what to do next. And then she opened her mouth and began to sing and, in spite of everything, he felt a thrill of excitement as that first note broke free. He sat back in his seat, listening as the soaring sound poured from her slender throat, and he felt another unwanted stir of his senses. So her reputation was founded on real talent and not just hype, he recognised—his eyes fixed with reluctant admiration to the sway of her hips, which moved in perfect time to the music.

The set passed in a blur. She sang of love and loss. She slung her head back as if in silent ecstasy and once again Titus felt that familiar tightening at his groin. Her low voice faltered as the last song ended on a breathless little sigh, and he had to snap out of the spell she seemed to have cast on him. To stop imagining those amazing lips making sweet music all over his body and to remember who she really was. A marriage-busting, money-grabbing little bitch. What must it be like to be as ruthless as Roxy Carmichael? he wondered. To be so desperate to cling onto the wealth she'd lost that she would steal another woman's husband in order to do so?

She ended the set abruptly—her half-closed eyes fluttering open after the last song as if she had just awoken from a dream and was surprised to find herself in the small and stuffy club. Still blinking, she obeyed the half-hearted applause by launching into one soulful encore—but the memorable tune sounded bizarre in the small and tacky setting of the Kit-Kat Club. And just as quickly she was gone, with a swish of the sparkly shirt and a glimpse of faded denim clinging to her bottom.

The pianist staggered off in the direction of the bar, the dusty velvet curtain came down and Titus rose to his feet and slipped on his coat, feeling oddly *dirty*. He could feel the sleazy fug of the place on his skin as he left the building, relieved to be able to suck in a breath of cold, crisp air as he walked round to the door at the back of the club.

His knock brought a heavy, middle-aged woman to the door, her hooded eyes flicking over him. 'Can I help you?'

'I hope so,' said Titus softly. 'I'm here to see Roxy Carmichael.'

'Is she expecting you?'

He shook his head. 'Not exactly.'

The woman's jowly face frowned with sharp scrutiny. 'Are you from the press?'

Titus curved his lips into a sardonic smile. Had centuries of privileged lineage resulted in him looking like a *journalist*? he wondered acidly. He shook his head. 'Most emphatically, no. I am not from the press.'

'Well, she says she's not taking any callers,' said the woman flatly.

'Are you sure?' Titus withdrew a slim leather wallet from his pocket and slickly peeled off a note, before sliding it into her unresisting hand. 'Why don't you ask her again...nicely?'

The woman seemed to hesitate for a moment before snatching the note and stuffing it in the pocket of her dress. 'I can't promise you anything,' she said ungraciously, jerking her head to indicate that he should follow her.

Stepping inside and shutting the stage door behind him, Titus was quickly enveloped in the gloom of the backstage area. He knew that he could have waited. Gone to see Roxanne Carmichael in the morning and delivered his crushing blow to her in the cold light of day and on his own territory. But his blood was fired up and he wanted to finish this off tonight. Besides, he was a man who never liked waiting—and now that he had control of the family estate it meant he never had to.

The woman in the floral dress had come to a halt and was now rapping on a dressing-room door.

'Who is it?' called a breathy voice he instantly recognised as that of Roxy Carmichael and something about its sensual undertones made his skin prickle with undeniable desire. But he stood hidden in the shadows as the door was pushed open and light streamed out from a shabby dressing room.

'It's Margaret,' said the woman, her hand moving around in her pocket as if she was checking the note he'd just given her was still there.

From her position at the mirror where she had been wiping the last of the gunky stage make-up from her face, Roxanne swivelled round in the chair, trying not to look dispirited. But it wasn't easy. It hadn't been the greatest evening in the world. There was nothing worse than playing in a half-empty club to an audience which was full of drink. The Kit-Kat Club seemed to be on the decline and she knew that her singing spot had failed to revitalise audience figures. Hadn't the management told her so just that very morning—in a grim message underpinned with the unspoken warning that lack of success would not be tolerated?

She told herself that it wasn't personal— that the music industry had always been this way. She just happened to have been very fortunate at the start of her career and she shouldn't forget that. But she was tired. Bone-tired. With an aching kind of emptiness which wouldn't shift and a horrible tickle at the back of her throat which wouldn't seem to go away.

Stifling a yawn, she looked at the woman in the floral dress who was standing in the doorway with an expectant look on her face and she forced a smile. 'Yes, what is it, Margaret?'

'There's a gentleman here who says he wants to see you.'

A gentleman? Roxanne deposited the damp piece of cotton wool on the battered dressing table and gave a wry smile. Once, there had been thousands of people who had clamoured at stage doors to see her. Men who wanted to go to bed with her, and young girls who had looked up to her for no reason she'd ever been able to work out. Squads of security people had been employed to keep those crowds at bay—but not any more. These days, visitors were few and far between and those that did make it past the stage door were greeted with suspicion. She found herself wondering if her father had turned up out of the blue—with yet another ridiculous scheme for making her 'comeback'. Her mouth tightened. As if she would ever consider letting *him* be a part of it—no matter how much her career could do with a lift. She thought about the dwindling audiences and the ever-more seedy venues and her heart twisted painfully in her chest. Because sooner or later she was going to have to take a tough, hard look at her future and ask herself how much longer she was going to tolerate being kicked back.

'Did he give his name?' she asked. 'Is he from the press?'

Margaret shrugged. 'He says he's not. And he doesn't look like a journalist. He looks…well…' she lowered her voice '…*handsome.*'

Roxanne suppressed a shudder. There was possibly only one thing worse than some journalist wanting to do a 'Where Are They Now?' feature—and that was a man who might have decided that she was still attractive enough to pursue. She gave a cynical shake of her head. 'I'm not interested in pretty boys, Margaret.'

'And *rich,*' murmured the older woman, like a bounty hunter.

At this, Roxy stilled—because some fantasies were too deeply ingrained to get rid of, no matter how crazy they might seem. Was it possible that her dream could still come true? That some wealthy impresario had been sitting in the audience listening to her singing and decided that he wanted to take a chance on her? Someone who had recognised that she still had a talent which burned brightly and which it was a crying shame to waste. And if that were the case, then surely it wouldn't hurt her to turn on the charm, would it?

Smoothing down her hair, she injected a note of warmth into her voice. 'Then why don't you send him in?' she said.

Titus had heard every word of the brief interchange and, although it shouldn't have surprised him, still it made his mouth harden. What had he expected—that she'd be proud enough to turn away some unknown caller who had turned up at the end of her set? Of course not. Just the mention of money had made her voice quiver with eagerness. Some women would sell themselves for money, he reminded himself, and this was one of them. Swallowing down the sour taste of disgust, he stepped forward.

'You can go in—' Margaret began, but Titus had already brushed past her and walked into the tiny dressing room.

Still seated, Roxy widened her eyes as a tall figure entered the cramped confines of the room. A hundred conflicting messages buzzed around in her head as he quietly shut the door behind him and for a moment she felt positively *weak*. She was aware of an immense power, which seemed to spark off him like electricity—and of something else, too. Something she'd almost forgotten about until she met his icy stare for the first time.

Desire.

She swallowed. A desire which was the last thing she wanted, or needed. It began to scorch like wildfire around her veins and suddenly the cramped room felt *claustrophobic*. She wanted to get out—far away from the way he was making her feel. She wanted to run a million miles from that bright grey gaze which was boring through her and making her heart perform an erratic dance. 'I don't remember telling you to close the door,' she said sharply.

Titus looked down at her—a hard smile on his lips as he registered the automatic darkening of her eyes in a response to him which was entirely predictable. He knew what he had—and what he had was something which made women fall at his feet like ninepins. He didn't exploit it, but sometimes he used it. 'Maybe you don't want the whole club hearing what I have to say,' he countered softly.

Roxy was about to tell him that she didn't tolerate silken threats coming from complete strangers, but suddenly she was finding it difficult to speak. She didn't know if it was his looks or his manner, or that cool, privileged accent which marked him out as aristocratic. But whatever it was, it was potent enough to make the words freeze in her throat. She let her gaze linger on him and somehow she couldn't seem to drag it away again.

He must have been about six feet two—although his posture made him seem taller. Clad in a dark cashmere coat designed to keep out the worst of the bitter winter night, she'd never seen anyone with quite so much *presence*. And that was a pretty big admission considering she'd spent her life working in an industry where charisma was the common currency...

His body would have made most women take a second look, and so would the expensive clothes which sat so comfortably on it. But women were usually more interested in faces—and his was the most arresting face she had ever seen. High cheekbones looked as if they had been chiselled by a master sculptor—their hard lines contrasting with the sensual contours of his unsmiling lips. His dark hair was the rich, tawny colour of burnt copper. Like a lion's mane, she found herself thinking. But his King-of-the-jungle likeness didn't stop at his hair. He carried himself with the effortless grace of a powerful predator—as if everything he surveyed through those cold eyes were his.

Roxy didn't react to his unsmiling scrutiny—at least, not outwardly. Her heart might have started fluttering with instinctive response to his outrageously alpha qualities, but he would never know that. She was good at keeping her feelings hidden. No, scrub that—she was an *expert*. She'd dealt with enough men in the past to know that they were all the same. That inevitably they had only one thing on their mind—and once they'd got it, you were history. So she certainly wasn't about to start panicking because some expensive-looking posh boy had walked in here, threatening to throw his weight around.

Deliberately, she turned her back on him and stared into the mirror as she wiped the scarlet lipstick from her lips with a blob of cotton wool. Because in that moment she knew that this man was no impresario. 'Isn't it polite to introduce yourself before you march into a woman's dressing room?'

Titus wasn't used to people turning away from him, especially not when their eyes had just been devouring him. He frowned. 'My name is Titus Alexander,' he said, watching her reflection closely to see if there were any signs of recognition, but no. She just carried on calmly wiping that garish lipstick from her mouth. And suddenly he found himself wondering what those lips might taste like beneath his. Whether they'd be able to inflict as much magic on his body as they'd done with the microphone, when she'd started to sing.

'What can I do for you, Mr Alexander?' she asked, in a bored tone.

Titus didn't bother correcting the fundamental mistake she was making about his title. Past experience had taught him that it was best to keep that particular fact hidden for as long as possible. Especially from women. 'I want to talk to you.'

'So talk.'

'And I'd prefer it if we were face to face.'

Her eyes met his in the mirror. 'Why?'

Because your eyes are so incredibly blue that I want to see them up close, he found himself thinking—before ruthlessly quashing the random thought. She was a fallen star, a cuckold and a money-grabber—and he was about to call time on her latest little scam. 'Call me old-fashioned, but I'd prefer not to have to address your back,' he drawled.

Her lips now bare of the startling colour she always wore to perform, Roxy slowly turned back to face him. 'How's that?' she questioned sarcastically.

Titus felt that same hard aching at his groin and for a moment he wished he'd kept his mouth shut. Because now his attention was once again distracted by her breasts. They were pushing blatantly against the sequin-sprinkled top in a way which seemed to be silently begging him to touch them. With an effort, he tore his gaze away and stared instead into the sapphire brilliance of her eyes. 'I believe you know Martin Murray?'

Roxy shrugged. 'I know a lot of people.'

'You know him rather well, I believe,' suggested Titus.

She registered his soft insinuation but she didn't respond to it. She didn't have to justify herself to privileged men who gate-crashed her dressing room. 'That's none of your business.'

'Actually, it is my business.'

Roxy threw the last wodge of cotton wool into the bin and rose to her feet, realising that she was still wearing her too-high stage shoes. 'Look, it's late, I'm tired and I want to go home. So why don't you cut to the chase and tell me what you're doing, marching in here and asking me all sorts of questions with that…that *judgemental* air you seem to have?'

'Maybe because I have the right to be judgmental,' he retorted. 'Since you happen to be illegally subletting one of my apartments.'

Roxy screwed her nose up, but something in his expression had made her pulse start to quicken. 'Don't talk rubbish,' she snapped. 'I've never seen you before in my life. You're not my landlord.'

'You don't think so?'

'I know so. Or rather, I know my landlord.'

'You live in the top-floor apartment of a large house in Notting Hill Gate, right?'

How the hell did he know that? Another wave of apprehension prickled over her skin, but Roxy hid it with a defiant look. 'Have you been stalking me?'

At this, Titus gave a low laugh. 'In your dreams, sweetheart. You think I'm the kind of man who needs to stalk *any* woman—let alone some second-rate singer who's fallen on times so hard that she's reduced to working in a dump like this?'

Something inside her retracted painfully but still Roxy didn't react. She was damned if she would let him see how much his words hurt. Or how much they had hit home. Instead, she managed another defiant stare. 'Then how come you know where I live?'

'I just told you. Because I happen to own the apartment you live in. In fact, I own the entire house,' he added.

Roxy felt the weight of her long hair brushing against a neck still sheened with sweat after her performance. 'No, you don't,' she croaked. 'You can't possibly. Martin owns it.'

'Is that what he told you?' enquired Titus idly. 'Was he pretending to be wealthy when he was trying to get you into bed?' His voice lowered with exasperation. 'Didn't it occur to you that he might be lying? Because that's what married men do. They lie to their wives and they lie to their mistresses. The wives usually mind because they have their family to think of—but the mistresses know it's all part of the whole sordid game. And so they overlook it—as they overlook so much else.' His grey eyes bored into her with undisguised contempt. 'Because in my experience, women who try to steal another woman's husband have no morals, nor any scruples either.'

Stuffing her hands deep into the pockets of her jeans so he wouldn't see they were trembling, Roxy shook her head. 'I've never tried to steal another woman's husband!'

'No?' His dark eyebrows shot up towards the tawny thickness of his hair. 'You just let him set you up in some kind of tawdry love nest?'

'It isn't like that!'

'I'm not interested in what it's "like",' he snapped. 'The only thing I'm interested in is that one of my employees has been illegally renting you one of my apartments and I want you out!'

'Your…employee?' Roxy echoed, racking her brains for some kind of recognition, but there was none. Titus was a pretty unforgettable name and she'd never heard Martin Murray mention it before. 'I've never heard of you, Mr Alexander. For all I know, you could be a complete fantasist.'

'You think so? Then maybe this might help convince you that what I'm saying is genuine.' Titus extracted a business card from the pocket of his cashmere overcoat and held it out towards her.

Removing her hand from the pocket of her jeans, Roxy took it, instantly aware of the expensive quality of the card—as expensive as everything else about him. Embossed black letters stood proud on the costly cream surface and as her eyes focused on it properly she experienced a strange, lurching feeling as the letters formed themselves into words.

Titus Alexander, Duke of Torchester.

The letters blurred again and suddenly her knees felt wobbly. It had been a long time since she'd eaten—she never liked to take food close to a performance—and in any other circumstances she might have slumped down in the chair, in shock. But some instinct told her that would be dangerous. That *he* would be dangerous if she showed any sign of weakness. She looked up into his cold eyes, her heart still racing. 'You're…you're the Duke of Torchester?'

'Yes, I'm the Duke of Torchester,' he drawled. 'And my late father employed your lover, Martin Murray, as his accountant. Starting to get your memory back are you, Miss Carmichael? Does my name ring a bell?'

Of course it rang a bell! Roxy nodded, willing her face to remain calm. It was imperative that she held onto her poise. To act as if she didn't care—because she remembered everything she'd ever heard about the aristocratic young Duke.

He's a ruthless bastard.

He was born with a silver spoon in his mouth.

Women love him.

Roxy's eyes were drawn to the unsmiling perfection of his mouth and the grey ice of his eyes and thought that, yes, women probably did love him. She could imagine it would be easy to fall for someone who had the looks and lineage of Titus Alexander. And equally easy to imagine him inflicting pain and heartbreak on any female who was stupid enough to do so.

'I don't understand,' she said flatly.

'No?' His tawny-dark eyebrows rose again in arrogant question. 'What *precisely* is perplexing you?'

'It's Martin's flat.'

'Is that what he told you?'

Roxy nodded, but even as he asked the question she began to understand all the things which had never really added up before. Why Martin had always insisted she pay her rent in cash. And why he had instructed her to tell anyone who asked that she was simply 'house-sitting'. She stared into Titus's grim face and it came as a shock to realise that she believed the word of this arrogant aristocrat above a man she'd known for years. 'That's what he told me.'

'Well, he was lying,' he iced out. 'A lying cheat of an accountant who my father made the mistake of trusting. Only my father is no longer around—and Martin Murray no longer works for my family. I'm in charge now and I intend clearing up the mess which your lover has made of the estate.' His grey eyes glittered dangerously. 'An estate which will no longer provide a refuge for wasters and chancers. So I want you out by the end of the week.'

Roxy felt a paralysing fear begin to well

up inside her and she fought successfully to dampen it down. Because fear was an emotion she was familiar with and she'd learnt that the only way to conquer it was to face it head-on. She knew that the moment you gave into it, you would be lost and that was *not going to happen*. Not with this arrogant posh-boy who had just marched into her dressing room with his inbuilt sense of entitlement. Clearing her throat, she tried to make her voice sound as cool as his. 'I don't think it works quite like that. I think the law states that you'll need to give me more notice than one week.'

Titus flattened his lips into an angry line as a slow rage began to flare up inside him. How *dared* she try to defy him? He thought about how his father had betrayed his mother, with a mistress as ruthless as this foxy-looking singer. He thought about the woeful state of the estate's finances and the way her crooked accountant of a boyfriend had been creaming off huge amounts for himself. Her *married* boyfriend, he thought in disgust.

He knew that his rage was disproportionate to her crime of having questionable morals, but Titus didn't care. Sometimes a person just happened to be in the wrong place at the wrong time—and Roxanne Carmichael was that person.

'The law isn't on your side,' he said silkily. 'Because you've been breaking it.'

She lifted her eyes up to his in genuine appeal. 'But I didn't know that.'

'I don't give a damn what you knew or what you didn't know,' he snapped, steeling himself against the brilliance of her gaze. 'And I'm not sure I'd believe you no matter how much you protest. The word of a woman who can cold-bloodedly sleep with a married man doesn't count for very much. So I want you—and every one of your tawdry possessions—out of my property by the end of the week. Do you understand *that*, Miss Carmichael?'

CHAPTER TWO

ALL the way home on the lurching night-bus, Titus Alexander's words burned into Roxy's memory. The wounding vitriol he had just directed against her had been bad enough but, unfortunately, there was an equally disturbing blot on her memory.

Despite the fear which was chewing her up inside, she couldn't shift the image of his towering presence and the tawny, dark hair, which had made her think of a lion. All she could see was a pair of hard, sensual lips and the brooding gleam of his grey eyes and once again she felt the distracting shiver of desire.

Cursing herself for the shallow nature of her thoughts, she forced herself to concentrate on what really mattered.

That if Titus Alexander was true to his

*word—she would soon be out on the street
with nowhere to go!*

Did he really have the power to kick her
out of the beautiful apartment which had
felt like the first real home she'd ever had?
Knotting her fingers tightly together, she
stared out of the window as late-night London passed in a blur.

The bus rumbled through Soho, dis-
charging various drunks along the way,
and then it skirted Hyde Park and headed
towards Holland Park. This was the point
of the journey when Roxy usually heaved
a huge sigh of relief and revelled in the
peace which came from staring out at the
wide open space which nestled so unexpectedly in the heart of the city. But not
tonight. Tonight her head was full of unwanted thoughts and the memory of those
judgmental pewter eyes as they had iced
over her. He had looked at her as if he really *despised* her. As if she were something
nasty that he had stepped in. And nobody
had ever looked at her quite like that before, even though she had lived a life which
had had more than its fair share of drama.

Stepping from the bus onto one of Notting Hill's premier tree-lined streets, she let herself into the vast, six-storey stuccoed house and climbed the stairs to her top-floor apartment. She tried telling herself that the arrogant Duke had been bluffing—but she couldn't keep up the pretence of believing that for long. Because deep down she knew he hadn't been bluffing. Even worse, she recognised now that she had been a fool of the first order. She had believed Martin Murray when he'd come up with his unbelievably generous offer. She had believed him because it had suited her to do so. Because she had been left without a penny of the vast fortune she'd made during her days with The Lollipops.

Yet if she'd stopped to think about it for more than a second, she would have realised that none of this had ever really made sense. As if Martin would own a huge apartment like this and then rent it out to her for such a ridiculously low rent. But she had let him, hadn't she? She'd closed her mind as to *why* he'd chosen to be so 'generous' and, instead, she had buried her head in the sand and just got on with it, because it had seemed like a lifeline thrown to her in an increasingly turbulent world.

It had been the first decent place she'd lived in since the fortune she'd acquired during her girl-band days had been lost in such spectacular style by her father. She'd gone from a six-bedroomed house in Surrey on glitzy St George's Hill—with its obligatory swimming pool and the cachet of knowing that John Lennon had once lived two streets away—to a series of ever-more shabby apartments. She'd downsized and downsized until all her worldly goods had been reduced to little more than the contents of a single suitcase. And hadn't her battered spirit found a blissful kind of refuge here in this glorious tree-lined street? Somewhere where she could just close the door on the rest of the world and lose herself in dreams of a brighter future.

Her last place had been a horrible bedsit above a dry-cleaning shop and she'd been paranoid that the fumes would affect her voice. But she hadn't had a lot of choice. She needed to be in London because that was where the work was—but living in London was prohibitively expensive. And lonely. Though maybe her other job contributed to the loneliness. Cleaning people's houses didn't provide colleagues and it didn't pay particularly well—but at least it gave her the flexibility to be able to carry on with her singing. And singing was her life. It was all she had left. The only real thing she had to hang onto.

She closed the door behind her and went into the bathroom to start running a bath, telling herself that she had come through things much worse than this. She had to keep positive and keep going—and by morning she would have discovered a solution to this particular problem.

But after a sleepless night the morning presented her with more than the worry of whether Titus Alexander would be as ruthless as he had implied. Her throat was tickly and sore—and felt as if someone had coated it with sandpaper. It was the professional singer's nightmare and when she tried a practice note, she heard the terrifying sound of her voice cracking. Roxy shivered. There were things she could put up with and things she could not—and losing her voice came in the latter category. In a panic she prepared a concoction of lemon and honey and hot water, which she cradled as she sat by the big window and dialled Martin Murray's number.

She never called him these days—although sometimes he rang her with that whiny note in his voice as he tried to get her to have dinner with him. But there was no whininess in his voice now—just an oddly furtive tone as he picked it up on the second ring.

Gone was the teasing flirtation which usually edged his words. 'Roxy,' he said warily. 'This is a surprise.'

'I've had a visitor,' she said flatly.

There was a pause. 'Go on.'

'Titus Alexander came to my dressing room.'

An odd, ugly note entered his voice. 'And?'

Roxy swallowed. 'And not only did he inform me that I was illegally subletting *his* apartment—he also told me that I had to be out by the end of the week.'

She waited. And waited. But what had she expected? That Martin Murray would tell her that the Duke was lying through his teeth? That she was safe and nothing was going to change? No, she hadn't thought that for a minute, though maybe she had hoped—a foolish hope which withered the moment she heard the accountant's answer.

'Not my problem, I'm afraid, Roxy. I'm having to deal with my own stuff—like finding myself unemployed for the first time in fifteen years. Made "redundant" by that arrogant young upstart Torchester.'

Roxy didn't waste words by asking why he had lied to her. She knew *exactly* why he had lied to her—and exactly why she had turned a blind eye to it. There was only one question she needed to ask and deep down she had known the answer all along.

'Do you think he means it?'

At this he gave a laugh she'd never heard before. It was the sound of bitter cynicism cloaked with a kind of hollow resignation. 'You bet your sweet ass he means it. The man is ruthless. I'd start looking round for a new place if I were you.'

Her hand was trembling as she put the phone down, knowing that she had no right to apportion blame. That the only person she could blame was herself. It was nothing to do with Martin Murray that she had no money for a deposit. That was *her* stuff. Her stuff and her stubbornness in refusing to give up on her dream of making it back to the big time. A dark spectre of fear hovered over her but she batted it away. She could work it out. She'd just have to see if she could find a small room in a house somewhere—maybe with a few light cleaning duties or child-care thrown in, which would guarantee a rock-bottom rent. Surely places like that existed?

But her sore throat became a hacking cough and she felt too weak to look around for somewhere new. She barely had the strength to drag herself off to one of her regular cleaning jobs in one of the big houses on Holland Park. Unfortunately, the Italian footballer's wife who was normally so sweet took one horrified look at her and said that she couldn't risk Roxy giving her cold to the children and that she needed to go straight back home.

In truth, Roxy couldn't blame her because this was beginning to feel like more than a cold—and it was getting worse by the minute. She felt too ill to get out of bed the next morning, and as panic began to mount that people would think her unreliable the week began to slip away.

She got the news that she'd lost her regular singing spot at the Kit-Kat Club on an icy morning when she was at her lowest ebb. They told her that they were sorry, but she wasn't pulling in the punters in as they'd hoped she would. She'd known that they'd wanted her to dress up as she used to when she was in The Lollipops. To wear those same outrageous clothes and sing all those old, familiar songs. But she couldn't do it. To try to recreate the past felt like a backward step and a betrayal—because she wasn't that person. Not any more.

Getting the sack felt like the final blow, yet somehow she managed to keep the tears at bay. It was that old self-preservation thing again, because she suspected that once she started crying she might never stop—and what good would that do her?

Forcing herself to be practical, she managed to make it round to the chemist to buy some paracetamol, but her legs felt so cotton-woolly that it seemed to take forever to get back home again. And all the time she kept wondering how she was going to manage. Whether the disapproving Duke of Torchester had meant what he'd said.

She leaned against the iron railings, so busy trying to catch her breath that for a moment she didn't notice the huge suitcase sitting outside the front door and when she did, she blinked.

That was…

She blinked again.

That was *her* suitcase!

Walking slowly up the steps towards it, her gloved fingers trembling as she clicked the bulging case open, she swallowed down the salty taste of tears as she saw what was inside. Her jeans. Her sparkly stage tops. Her toiletries stuffed into that ancient soap-bag she'd had since her days with The Lollipops. And there, peeping out from among the other more functional clothes, were glimpses of her undies—bras and knickers, stuffed haphazardly into wherever there was a space.

Roxy snapped the case closed as dizzy yellow spots began to dance beneath her eyelids. And even though she knew it was completely pointless, she still attempted to wriggle her key into the front-door lock, which was mocking her with its brand-new shininess. It wouldn't fit, she thought frustratedly. It wouldn't fit and she knew exactly why.

'Roxanne?'

Roxy immediately recognised the cultured, feminine voice behind her—her heart sinking as she forced her head to turn to see that it was indeed Annabella Lang, the privileged trust-fund blonde who lived next door.

Unable to muster even a smile, Roxy nodded as she pulled her useless key away from the door. *Don't show your desperation*, she urged herself as she sucked in a deep, painful breath. 'Hello, Bella.'

'What is going on? Some goon was round here earlier changing all the locks on the door!'

Talk about stating the obvious, thought Roxy wearily. 'I'm moving,' she croaked.

But Annabella was clearly much more interested in something other than Roxy's housing difficulties. 'And *then*…' She paused dramatically, for effect. 'You'll never guess who came storming round, looking as if the world was about to end?'

'Who?' questioned Roxy, though she could tell from the other woman's sudden air of adulation just who that might be.

'Titus Alexander,' said Annabella, her eyes narrowing. 'The Duke of Torchester! I didn't realise you knew him! And I didn't realise he owned this house,' she finished accusingly.

Roxy didn't bother saying 'and neither did I'. Even if she'd wanted a conversation with Annabella, she didn't think she'd be coherent enough to make any sense right now, because her head had started pounding and her throat felt as if it were on fire.

She needed to get out of here and she needed to lie down before she fell down. 'I have to go,' she croaked.

'But go where?' asked Annabella, her voice sounding incredulous as she watched Roxy struggle to pick up the heavy case.

Perhaps if she hadn't been feeling so woozy, then Roxy might have invented a fictitious series of friends who'd be only too glad to let her sofa-surf until she found a place of her own. But she felt so low and defeated that she just blurted out the truth—not caring a jot about her battered pride or Annabella's horrified face.

'I'll find a hostel,' she mumbled. 'Just for the night.'

She began to haul her heavy suitcase down the street, not stopping until she reached the bus stop and was certain she was away from Annabella's pitying stare. And when the bright red double-decker bus stopped, she bought a ticket planning to travel as far away from this privileged area of West London as possible. Because she didn't belong here. Come to think of it, she didn't really belong anywhere.

Somehow she found a hostel, not caring that it was right by a busy Tube station or that to get there she had to pass three people sitting on a pavement, asking passers-by for money.

She just needed to sleep, that was all. In the morning she would feel better—and after that she would find somewhere to live. She wondered if the desperation showed on her face or whether it could be heard in her croaky voice—but something in her heart-felt appeal must have worked, because she was given a bed.

It was an iron bedstead with a lumpy mattress, in a dormitory with twenty other women—some of whom seemed to be withdrawing from alcohol. Their delusional screams about yellow ants pierced the night and ordinarily Roxy would have been terrified. But the pounding in her head was pretty much all she could think about right then—until she remembered that she'd left no forwarding address and that she was expecting a much-needed cheque. And that she wouldn't put it past the hateful Titus Alexander to throw it in the bin, out of spite.

With trembling fingers, she scrabbled around in her bag until she'd found the arrogant aristocrat's card, then fumbled him a text, before flopping back against the flat pillow.

She'd never felt so ill in her life. The walls were closing in on her. Her skin was growing hot. And just before her eyelids fluttered to a close, she cursed the tawny-headed man whose cruel behaviour had brought her here.

CHAPTER THREE

A FADED denim crotch swam into view and Roxy's heavy eyelids slowly fluttered open. Narrow hips framed the crotch like a prize exhibit at an art show and for a moment she was so disorientated that she simply stared at it. Slowly, she moved her gaze upwards to meet the shuttered gaze of Titus Alexander.

'You're awake, I see,' he remarked acidly.

Roxy blinked. She felt warm and comfortable and the room was strangely *quiet*. Yet she remembered going to sleep on a lumpy mattress with the sound of demented voices all around her. More memories began to crowd into her befuddled brain. The sleepless night which had turned into a sleepless day. The pounding in her head and the terrible aching in her throat—followed by the soaring bewilderment of a high fever when her skin had felt as icy as if she'd spent the night in the Arctic. The hostel!

Despite the restrictive heaviness of her limbs, she sat up in bed and her eyes narrowed in disbelief as she looked around. No, definitely not the hostel. She was in a huge room, with light streaming in from equally huge windows. Gone was the dormitory with its rows of sardine-packed beds—and in its place was a tranquil bedroom, decorated entirely in white. A crystal chandelier hung from the ceiling and the bed in which she was lying was covered with crisp and deliciously clean linen.

Roxy stared up at the Duke's striking aristocratic features, her heart pounding with confusion. 'Where am I?' she demanded.

'In my London home.'

'How did I get here?' she questioned, her voice rising on a slight note of hysteria.

'You don't remember?'

'If I remembered, then I wouldn't be asking, would I?'

Titus felt his mouth harden. Ungrateful little witch. He should have left her in the hostel where he'd found her! 'I brought you here,' he said flatly. 'You've been ill.'

Roxy slumped back against the billowy bank of pillows. Illness would explain this strangely weak and woozy feeling—but it didn't explain why Titus Alexander was standing next to the bed and glowering down at her. She stared at him suspiciously. 'What do you mean—you *brought* me here?'

'I mean,' said Titus, with a growing feeling of impatience that he should have to explain himself to her after all he'd done, 'that I went to the hostel where you were staying, to give you some letters which had been delivered for you. And that's when I found you delirious with fever and looking quite shockingly ill—with no proper medical care or attention. So I put you in my car and brought you back here.'

She blinked at him as more fragments of memory began to piece themselves together in her mind. She remembered feeling icy cold, but her body being drenched with sweat. At one point, her teeth had been chattering so loudly that she'd been afraid she might shatter them. There had been wild voices shouting out all around her— or had one of those voices been hers? And then someone picking her up. Someone very strong. She vaguely remembered slumping against a rock-hard chest as she'd been carried out of that scary place and put into a car. Her eyes narrowed as she met the Duke's cool expression.

'It was you. You rescued me,' she said slowly.

Titus gave a cynical laugh, because the last thing he needed was for her to start building schoolgirlish fantasies about an episode he would rather hadn't happened. 'I felt duty-bound to get you out since I felt partially responsible for you being there,' he growled. 'Though, of course, if you hadn't made such a complete mess of your life—then you wouldn't have been there in the first place. So I brought you back here and had my friend Guy Chambers look you over—'

'Look me over?' she breathed. 'What do you mean, *look me over*?'

'He's a doctor,' he answered as he read the suspicious look in her eyes. 'Not some kind of voyeur. He diagnosed you with pneumonia, he prescribed antibiotics and rest—and that's what you've been getting ever since.'

But she must have been getting more than rest, mustn't she? Her hair and body felt scented and clean and…Roxy placed her hand over her racing heart, only to encounter the slippery feel of silk against her fingers. Pulling the sheet away by a fraction, she stared down at the apricot sheen of a nightdress which must have cost a fortune. She could feel the delicate fabric brushing against her bare knees and the deep scoop of its low-cut back and she clutched onto the sheet as she looked at him with renewed suspicion.

'What am I wearing?' she demanded.

'What does it look like?' he growled, furious with his body's instant reaction to the provocative outline of her breasts.

'But I didn't arrive with a silk nightdress! I don't even *possess* a silk night-dress. Whose is it?'

'It's yours now. I had someone from the store deliver a few, the morning after you arrived—since you seemed to have only one of your own, which, frankly, was well past its sell-by date. And I decided that clothing you was better than seeing you naked, every time I walked past.'

'You mean you...you stripped me off and dressed me?' she demanded, her heart beginning a ragged thunder.

Titus gave a short laugh. 'Actually, I employed a nurse to do that. I haven't quite reached the point of dragging sick women back to my house so that I can have my wicked way with them.' He paused as he flicked his eyes over her. 'Added to which, I'm afraid that you're just not my type.'

Roxy's face didn't betray any kind of reaction, but stupidly his remark *hurt*. It was bad enough being made to feel like a complete waif and stray without it being implied that you were hideously unattract-ive. Anyway, it was obvious what sort of woman he would go for. A starchy aristocrat like Titus Alexander would be attracted to someone like Annabella, her ex-next-door neighbour, with her perfect pedigree and clothes which always looked like an upmarket uniform.

'Well, you're not my type either,' she said defensively, putting her hand over her mouth as she began to cough.

'Really? I'm crushed!'

'I don't go for toffee-nosed, stuck-up aristocrats who were born with a silver spoon in their mouth!'

'I suppose the fact that I'm single must also be a bit of a barrier,' he offered sarcastically. 'Because you seem to like the buzz of the forbidden. I can't think what else attracted you to my father's accountant. Was it just the cheap rent which won you over, or did his large beer-gut play a part in luring you into his bed?'

'I didn't go to bed with Martin Murray!' she snapped, but the effort of having a row with him was too much and she slumped back against the pillows to see him watching her from between narrowed eyes. 'How long have I been here?'

'Five days.'

Five days? Roxy's feeling of disorientation increased and it wasn't helped by her sudden acknowledgement of how long it had been since she'd been alone in a bedroom with a man. And the even more unwanted acknowledgement of just how sexy a man he was. His soft, dark sweater sleeves were rolled up to reveal hair-roughened arms and his jeans were close-fitting and faded. Effortlessly, they emphasised the narrow jut of his hips and the taut definition of his powerful legs. How weird it was to think that this man was actually a *Duke* when he looked more like some pin-up of a rock-star. 'That's a long time,' she observed, her skin prickling with unwanted awareness.

Tell me about it, Titus thought grimly. Five days of trying not to focus on that amazing body which had clung to him as he'd carried her inside on that frosty night. Or to remember the brief glimpse of her cherry-tipped nipples when she'd torn her nightdress off in the middle of her delirium. It had been that fever-fuelled gesture which had made him instantly decide that he needed a nurse there.

He cleared his throat, trying to ignore the fact that her hair was tumbling over her narrow shoulders or that those cherry nipples were now outlined by the silk of her nightgown. He shouldn't be thinking about what it would be like to explore all that soft and silken skin. She was trouble in every sense of the word and the thing he needed to do now was to get her out of here and out of his life. Only this time, for good.

'So how are you feeling?' he forced himself to ask.

Roxy gave a shrug, knowing that he wasn't interested in hearing her worries about what had been happening work-wise during the five days she'd been out of it. Or her concerns about what the cleaning agency would make of her unplanned absence. Her inbuilt survival system took over and she even managed a watery smile. 'Hungry.'

'Good.' He nodded, as if that was the first sensible word she'd uttered. 'So why

don't you get dressed and I'll fix you some
breakfast?'

Roxy nodded, hearing the note of closure
in his voice. No doubt he would send her
on her way after a hearty breakfast. A last
meal for the condemned woman. 'Okay.'

'You'll find your clothes in the wardrobe
over there,' he said abruptly, on his way out
of the bedroom. 'I hope you don't mind, but
I had them sent out to be laundered.'

What could she say—that he made her
feel a bit like some feral animal who'd
needed to be hosed down and disinfected?
Roxy waited until he'd gone before gingerly getting out of bed, but her legs felt
wobbly and she was decidedly weak as she
showered and washed her hair. She remembered losing her job at the Kit-Kat Club and
wondered what on earth she was going to
do. More importantly—where on earth she
was going to *go*? Pulling on a deliciously
fresh-smelling sweater, she wriggled into
her jeans—except that there wasn't much
wriggling to be done because they slipped
on much too easily. No woman ever wore
her jeans *this* big, she thought—adding a

belt to cinch them in as she wondered just how much weight she had lost.

She made the bed and tidied up the room, but she knew she couldn't keep putting off going downstairs and facing her bleak future. Her heart was pounding as she followed the sound of clashing pots to find Titus cooking breakfast.

The kitchen was situated right at the back of the house and contained all the usual luxury components of a no-money-spared environment. There was a big, scrubbed oak table and a beautiful dresser crowded with china which looked scarily valuable. At the other end of the room, two squashy sofas overlooked a garden which was huge, by city standards. It was like one of those rooms featured in the lifestyle magazines you sometimes found lying around in the dentist's surgery. Only they didn't usually feature someone like Titus Alexander standing stirring something over a huge range.

It made an incongruous image to see the powerful aristocrat doing something so *domesticated* as cooking and for a moment

Roxy stood watching him, her feeling of trespassing growing by the minute. And not just of trespass... She found her eyes straying to the dark, beaten copper of his ruffled hair and the broad back which tapered down to a perfect bottom and once again she felt a powerful rush of lust. Did he have a lover? she wondered. And if so, wouldn't she have *minded* him giving some complete stranger house-room for nearly a week?

He must have heard her—or sensed her presence—because he turned round, his expression shuttered as he surveyed her.

'Sit down. I'm fixing you some eggs.'

She noticed he didn't bother asking her whether she *liked* eggs. 'Where's my phone?' she questioned as she sat down at the table.

'Eat first,' he said, walking over and sliding a plate of scrambled eggs towards her.

She didn't like his autocratic attitude one bit, but the sight of the food he'd placed in front of her stopped Roxy from saying so. She must have been hungrier than she'd thought because she gave a little moan of greed and ate every scrap, followed by two slices of toast and jam and a large cup of strong black coffee. When she'd finished, she looked up to find Titus leaning against the range, watching her—still with that shuttered expression on his face.

Suddenly the false intimacy of the scene made her feel a stupid pang of wistfulness and she wondered where *that* had come from. But the thoughts carried on coming, no matter how hard she tried to stop them. Was this what he did for his girlfriends? she found herself wondering. Cook them breakfast after spending the night making love to them? And would he make love as superbly as he scrambled eggs?

You bet he would.

'Better?' he questioned laconically.

'Much. Thank you. You cook a mean egg.' She forced a smile. 'Now, can I have my phone please?'

'Of course. Your handbag's over there, by the sofa.'

Slowly, Roxy got up from the table, her mind racing as she tried to work out what she was going to do. Could she throw herself on the mercy of one of her old bandmates? Tell them she'd reached rock-bottom and could they please give her a bit of respite while she sorted her life out? But Justina might still be involved with that tyrant of an Italian, mightn't she? Roxy doubted whether he'd welcome a semi-permanent house-guest which might cramp their sexual Olympics. And she hadn't heard from Lexi in ages.

Acutely aware of Titus Alexander's searing gaze, she withdrew her phone from her bag with trembling fingers, but she could see instantly that the screen was completely blank. Turning her back on him, she stared unseeingly out at the wintry garden as she went through the pantomime of punching out some numbers.

Closing her eyes, she clamped the phone to her ear, waiting for a moment or two before she started exclaiming in a bright voice, 'Justina, *hi*! It's Roxy. Yeah, yeah— I'm great. Great. Well, actually not so—'

But at that moment the phone was plucked from her hand and when she whirled round, it was to see Titus standing holding it, a grim expression on his face as his grey eyes bored into her.

'What do you think you're doing?' she demanded.

'Why are you pretending to have a conversation?'

'I'm not *pretending* to have a conversation!'

'Really? Then you must have communication skills beyond the reach of most mortals, Roxanne—since the phone battery happens to be *dead*!"

Roxy had been in enough tight corners in her life to know that you couldn't go wrong with the old truism of attack being the best form of defence. 'And how do you know that?' she raged. 'Have you been rifling through my handbag while I've been ill?'

'Believe me, sweetheart, I've got better things to do than go through your damned handbag,' he swore. 'I happen to know because just before it died, it kept ringing and ringing. I thought it might be something important—but it was just your lover trying to get hold of you.'

'My…lover?' questioned Roxy faintly.

'Murray.'

'How many times do I have to tell you?' she grated. 'That he is not and never has been my lover.'

'No? So how come he let you pay peanuts for your rent?'

Roxy hesitated as she met the accusatory glitter of his eyes. 'Because...because he was being kind to me, I suppose.'

At this, Titus gave a cynical laugh. 'Oh, come on, Roxanne, you're not that naive,' he said as he looked into her amazing blue eyes and thought how they could blind a man with their beauty. 'Ruthless businessmen like Murray aren't "kind" for no reason. The guy had the hots for you. And maybe you decided that humping him wasn't too high a price to pay to live in one of the smartest areas in London—even if he did have a wife at home. You wouldn't be the first woman to do it and you certainly won't be the last.'

'You're disgusting!' she spat back.

'Maybe I am.' His eyes narrowed. 'Or maybe I'm just speaking the truth and you can't bear to hear it. Unless you're denying that he wanted you?'

Again, Roxy hesitated. When those steely eyes were boring into her like that, it was difficult to look away—and she got the terrifying impression that he knew exactly what the set-up had been. Besides, she wasn't trying to impress him, was she? Who cared what Titus Alexander thought of her? It was what she thought of herself that mattered. 'Yes, he wanted me,' she admitted baldly.

'Of course he did. Let me guess,' he mused silkily. 'You didn't actually go to bed with him, but you left him dangling with the hope that one day you might?'

Roxy flushed as his words hit home with an accuracy which made her feel uncomfortable. She had told the accountant very firmly that she didn't date married men and that much was true. But most men had uncrushable egos, didn't they? Perhaps he had thought that persistence might wear away her resistance and perhaps it had suited her to let him think that.

'I can't control what goes on in people's minds,' she retorted.

And neither could he, thought Titus reluctantly. He couldn't even control what was going on in his own mind. Because why the hell was he looking at her calculating little face and wishing he could wipe away her defiance with a hard and punishing kiss? What was it about bad girls like Roxanne Carmichael, which always made men hunger for them? Angrily, he swallowed down the lump which seemed to have lodged in his throat—wishing it were as easy to rid himself of the hard aching in his groin.

'So what are you going to do now?' he questioned unsteadily, wishing he could just wave a wand and magic her out of his life.

His words brought with them an element of reality and feeling a bit wobbly again, Roxy quickly sat down on the sofa. 'I haven't decided,' she said, aware of how ridiculous she must sound. As if she had a million choices ahead of her instead of none at all. 'But first I need to get my phone working.'

'Superior communication skills suddenly failing you, Roxanne?' he mocked. 'Here, give me the charger.'

With shaky fingers she fumbled around in her handbag and handed it over to him, watching as he plugged it into the socket. She realised how shockingly easy it was to defer to him and wondered if people always did. Or did his natural dominance come as much from the power of his personality as from the title he had inherited?

He straightened up to meet her gaze. 'You can use my phone,' he said.

Realising that she had no choice, she took it—even though she hated the idea of him listening into her conversation. She punched out the number but could tell instantly from the tone of the woman who answered that things weren't good. In fact, that was the understatement of the year. Pressing the phone tightly to her ear, she hoped that Titus wouldn't hear the tirade of complaints which were now being launched against her. That she had let down several of their biggest clients by not bothering to show up for work.

'I've been ill,' she told the woman at the agency, praying that some small amount of sympathy would come floating her way. She glanced up to his grey eyes fixed on her and she felt a disconcerting shiver whispering its way up her spine. She cleared her throat and looked away from him. 'I've had…pneumonia.'

'Well, that's not our responsibility, I'm afraid. You should start looking after yourself properly. Stop burning the candle at both ends,' said the woman haughtily. 'Decide whether you want to be a cleaner or a singer—because clearly you can't do both. I'm sorry, Roxanne—but I can't take the risk of employing unreliable workers. Not with the calibre of clients we have here.'

Perhaps if Titus hadn't been standing there, then Roxy might have pleaded her case. Told the agency that she'd be available for any kind of work they cared to throw at her and she'd never let them down again.

But she recognised that she might not be able to stick to such a promise because at that moment she felt so weak that she wasn't sure she'd even be able to get up from the wretched sofa. She had no alternative but to say goodbye and terminate the connection, silently handing the phone back to Titus, who was still watching her in that curiously unsettling way. As if she were a member of some alien species who had decided to inhabit the body of a woman for the day.

'That didn't sound like a very fruitful conversation,' he observed.

'How very astute of you.'

'Who was it?' he demanded.

She reflected that accepting help and hospitality didn't really allow you to tell someone to mind their own business. And that it might do him good to realise how the other half lived. But there was a stupid streak of pride which made her reluctant to dispel her image of sultry songstress and confess to him the mundane truth of her existence. 'The cleaning agency, where I work. Worked,' she corrected hollowly.

His dark brows arrowed together. 'You're a *cleaner*?'

'A domestic facilitator, they call it nowadays. But the terminology is irrelevant, since they've just given me the sack.'

'But you've just been ill,' he objected.

'Apparently, I've just let down two of their biggest clients.'

'And can they do that—just let you go?'

'Who knows? But I'm hardly in a position to be able to take *Maid In Heaven* to court on grounds of unfair dismissal, am I, Titus?' She met his eyes and wondered if he could appreciate the exquisite sense of irony. 'I'm afraid that when you're the economic underdog, then people can behave pretty much how they please towards you.'

Titus narrowed his eyes at the barb behind her words. Yet he could hardly chastise her agency for their cold-heartedness, when he'd behaved in a similarly ruthless manner, could he? If he hadn't kicked her out on the street, then maybe none of this would have happened. He felt an unwilling twist of guilt. 'Have you got relatives you can go to?' he questioned.

'No.'

'What about your parents?'

'I said *no*,' she snapped.

He saw the stubborn tightening of her mouth. 'Then what are you going to do?'

Roxy shrugged as if she didn't really care, reminding herself that this wasn't the first time something like this had happened. She'd learnt to face the bad times and not to let them grind her down. But it didn't matter how much positive reinforcement she murmured to herself, that didn't solve her immediate problem of having nowhere to live. She glanced out of the window, where the morning's frost showed no sign of thawing.

'I don't know,' she said tonelessly as she watched a blackbird perch on the bare branch of a tree and wondered if that bird could possibly feel as lonely as she did right then.

Titus didn't know what made him suggest it. Whether it was the desolate way she spoke those words or whether it had more to do with the sudden tremble of her lips—an unconsciously erotic tremble, which made his heart begin to beat a little faster. Because he wanted her, he realised, his eyes reluctantly drawn to the way her sweater hugged her luscious breasts. And wanting her spelt trouble.

Yet he was beginning to realise that he couldn't just walk away and forget about her. He'd done that once before and look what had happened. He didn't particularly like her—and he certainly didn't trust her—but he could hardly kick her out on a bitterly cold winter's day, could he?

'You can come and work for me,' he said slowly.

Roxy blinked. 'For you?'

He shrugged. 'I have an estate in the country and I'm having a party there at the end of the month. We always employ extra staff whenever there's a big event on. I'm sure we can find space for an extra cleaner.'

The words screamed their way into her consciousness and Roxy flinched. *An extra cleaner.* Was that what she had become? She looked into his proud, aristocratic features and at that moment something inside her died. Or rather, her image of herself did, be-cause Titus Alexander clearly had no problem defining her by her humble job. From pop idol to skivvy in less than a decade.

She winced. Well, *damn him.* Damn him and his privileged life—he who had probably never done a proper day's work in his life. How she would have loved to turn around and tell him just what he could do with his lousy job, but it was a bleak day out there and she had nowhere else to go.

And she was a survivor, wasn't she? She'd come through far worse than this. Steeling herself against the speculative gleam in his grey eyes, she returned his cool gaze.

'When do I start?' she questioned carelessly.

CHAPTER FOUR

THE vintage Bentley drove slowly through the arched stone entrance and Roxy stared at the vast, rolling parkland ahead, which spread out as far as the eye could see. The light covering of frost on the grass made the setting look like some old-fashioned and very beautiful Christmas card. In the distance she could see the pale golden blur of a building—the biggest and grandest building she had ever seen. Surely that couldn't be his *house*?

Glad to have something to focus on other than the taut and muscular thighs of the man sitting next to her, Roxy widened her eyes. 'You *must* be joking,' she breathed.

Titus shot her a glance, noticing the way that the pale winter sunlight illuminated her dark-blonde hair. He supposed he should have been grateful that she'd slept for most of the long journey from London to Norfolk and that she hadn't been distracting him with her flippant comments. Yet when she was sleeping, her raw sexuality seemed to ooze from every pore of her amazing body. As if silently begging him to do what nature had conditioned a man like him to do to a woman like her. Each time they'd stopped at a traffic light, he had found himself turning to study her.

Her silky hair had been spread out over the leather headrest and her magnificent breasts had slowly risen and fallen with every breath she took. Her cushioned lips had been parted and her lashes had fanned the pale perfection of her cheeks. She'd managed to look both angelic and yet wickedly accessible—and he had been overcome by a lust so powerful that it had been as much as he could do not to have pulled her into his arms and started kissing her.

And wouldn't that be the worst idea in the world? To seek carnal comfort with a woman like her?

With an effort, he returned his attention to the long drive which led up to the house.

'I don't remember making a joke,' he said repressively.

'I don't mean a literal joke,' said Roxy, because wasn't it simpler to concentrate on the architectural magnificence of his home, rather than on the disapproving presence beside her? 'I mean, you didn't tell me that you lived in what is practically a *palace*! Titus, it's absolutely *massive*! And surely that's…' Her eyes narrowed as she saw a bright gleam on the horizon which could only mean one thing. 'That's not the sea over there, is it?'

'Indeed it is,' he answered, his mouth hardening as he heard the avaricious excitement in her voice. 'We have our own beach.'

'Your own beach,' she repeated and then, because she was so taken aback by the sheer scale of the place, she spoke without really thinking. 'I wonder how much a place like this would cost on the open market?'

'I hope I never have to find out,' he snapped.

'You mean you'd never sell it?'

'I mean I can't sell it, even if I wanted to.' He nodded briefly at the gardener who was touching a deferential finger to his brow as the big Bentley drove slowly past. Titus knew that many people tried to calculate the extent of his wealth, though, unlike her, most were too polite to do it out loud. But there again—what would someone like her know of aristocratic life?

'Actually, it's not mine to sell. I'm just the custodian who looks after it for future generations. That responsibility is the price I pay for having so many privileges.'

She peered through the wintry light as she thought she saw a church in the distance. Surely he didn't have his *own church*, as well? 'Well, if you're expecting me to feel any sympathy for you, then I'm afraid you'll have a long wait. You could accommodate half of England in a place this big.'

Titus gripped the steering wheel as he stared at the splendour of his ancestral home. At times she could be so vulgar! His attention was momentarily distracted by her crossing one slim, denim-clad leg over the other and once again he felt the potent kick of lust. Was it unconscious or deliberate—that powerful sexual allure she seemed to exude? For the first time he began to wonder how she might fit in with the rest of the staff—and whether this worldly urban singer would adapt to the isolation of his vast Norfolk estate.

Yet, inevitably, he felt some of the tension escape from his body as he drove towards the glowing golden brickwork of Valeo Hall. He might simply be the ancient building's temporary custodian and it might bring back bitter memories of his fractured childhood—but it was still home. Still the place where he felt most free. Where he could walk through the vast grounds of the estate and lose himself in the beauty of nature.

'I'll take you straight up to the great house,' he said. 'And you can get to know your way around.'

Roxy nodded, trying to get her head around the fact that this was going to be her new place of employment. 'How many people work here?' she said.

He sighed. 'These days there's only a skeleton staff, I'm afraid.'

'You mean they're all dead?'

'That's not even funny, Roxanne.'

'Then why are you laughing?'

Titus subdued the hint of a smile. 'What I mean is that the aristocracy have had to make cuts, just like everyone else.'

'Oh, dear.' She mimed playing a violin. 'My heart bleeds. Couldn't you just sell off a few thousand acres if you're broke? By my calculation, that would still leave you with a few thousand more.'

'I think you've made your point,' he said coolly. 'I thought you wanted to find out about my staff—as opposed to the minutiae of my property portfolio. You'll answer to Vanessa—she's the housekeeper. There's a cook and various kitchen staff. There are also ground staff and secretarial staff and several cleaners—I have no idea of exact numbers. But I'm sure you'll soon get to know them all.'

'Right,' said Roxy, resisting the temptation she'd been fighting ever since she'd woken up and turning in her seat to look

at him properly. Her initial assessment of
him had been an accurate one. He really
was the most charismatic man she'd ever
met and she wondered if he'd always been
that way. She tried to imagine what he must
have been like as a little boy—but it wasn't
easy to imagine Titus as being in any way
little. Had he always had that wayward lock
of thick, tawny hair brushing against his
neck? And did women always feel an urge
to brush it away and to place their lips there
instead? She bet they did.

Rather self-consciously, she cleared her
throat in an effort to distract herself. 'So
what's it like, growing up surrounded by
staff?' she asked.

Titus slowed the Bentley down. 'You
must have had people working for you during your heady days as a star.'

She tried not to notice the way the mus-
cles of his thigh tensed when he pressed on
the clutch or the sarcasm which had hardened his voice when he said 'star' like that.
'Yes, I did—but they were employed by the
record company, or by whichever hotel we

happened to be staying in. I didn't have any staff of my own.'

'But you must have had a manager.'

'My father acted as my manager,' she said tonelessly.

He heard the chill which had crept into her voice. 'But he's no longer around?'

'He's not dead, if that's what you mean.'

'It wasn't.'

Roxy stared down at her unpainted fingernails, aware that two of them were broken. His unspoken question hung on the air but she guessed he was too well brought up to say it. *Why couldn't you go to your father for help? Why did you tell me you didn't have any relatives?*

'He's around,' she elaborated reluctantly. 'But he's no longer my manager and he wouldn't be, even if I had need of one—which I don't. I don't really see him very much at all these days.'

'And why's that?'

His unexpected question surprised her so much that she found herself answering it. Because for a moment then, he sounded as if he was actually *interested*. As if she

was more than just an unnecessary burden
he'd been forced to carry.

'His succession of increasingly young
girlfriends doesn't exactly help smooth the
father-daughter relationship,' she said. 'But
things have never been quite the same between us since he lost my entire fortune
due to some pretty dire investments.'

'Ouch,' he said softly.

Roxy shrugged. 'Yes, it was pretty painful at the time—but you get used to it. Easy
come, easy go,' she recited, with a care-
lessness which she had deliberately culti-
vated over the years. Because what was the
point in lamenting something you couldn't
change? 'But anyway, that's enough about
me. What family do you have?'

Titus let the Bentley crawl along at a
snail's pace. If it had been anyone else, he
probably would have changed the subject.
And if it had been anyone else, they would
probably have let him. But Roxanne Carmichael was different, he recognised—and
not just because she had the rather cocky
confidence which came from having once
received mass acclaim. She was different

because of the circumstances surrounding her arrival at his house.

She wasn't just someone who had applied through the usual channel of an advertisement placed in the back of a genteel magazine. *He* had brought her here—and thus a rather unusual bond had formed between them. Which meant that he couldn't be as dismissive to her as he would with any other junior member of staff—none of whom would have dreamed of asking him such a personal question. And she was going to be living here, he reminded himself. Inevitably she was going to find out more about him. So why not cut out the middleman and let her hear it from him for a change?

'My father died eighteen months ago, which was when I inherited the title. Before that, I was living in Paris as a humble earl.'

'I can't imagine you being a humble anything.'

'Should I take that as a compliment?' He saw the look on her face and gave a sardonic smile. 'No, I didn't think so.'

'And is your mother still alive?'

'She is,' he answered. 'She lives in Scotland now.'

'Oh? Why not here?'

He cut the engine even though they were still some distance away from the house, but he knew that the moment he approached one or more of the servants would appear to greet him. 'Because my mother divorced my father many years ago,' he said. 'When she discovered that he'd been having a long affair with the woman who was later to become my stepmother.'

Roxy registered the contempt in his voice as he said the word *stepmother* and suddenly his behaviour became a little more understandable. Did his father's extra-marital affair explain why he'd been so quick to condemn her when he thought she'd been seeing Martin Murray?

'And your stepmother still lives here, does she?' she questioned, wondering what on earth the atmosphere was going to be like if he said yes.

'She does not. She moved on to pastures new when my father became infirm. Fortunately, I was able to persuade him to dissolve the marriage before he died.' His tone became cold and steely. 'So although he was cuckolded and made a fool of—at least she wasn't able to make some outrageous claim on the estate.'

The ruthlessness which had hardened his voice didn't surprise her—because hadn't she encountered it herself? What a difficult man he could be. But he was also a very charismatic man, with an allure she was finding it almost impossible to ignore. And that was crazy. She was sensitive enough to realise that, while he might fancy her, he certainly didn't *like* her. And she'd be wise to put any romantic thoughts right out of her head and get this relationship on a more formal footing.

So start taking control right now!

'I feel I ought to thank you,' she said stiffly. 'For rescuing me from that awful hostel and giving me a job.'

He shrugged. 'Let's just call it cause and effect, shall we? It was my fault that you were in the hostel in the first place.'

Roxy shook her head. It might make her feel better to blame him for everything that had happened to her, but it wasn't very fair. 'Not really. I'd been feeling ropey for days. I should have gone to see a doctor myself.'

That was generous of her, he conceded—watching as she twisted her long hair into a single plait and tied it with a scrunchy. Watching as it tumbled over the luscious swell of her breasts. With an effort, he re-directed his attention to the towering splendour of his ancestral home.

'Look,' he said softly as he brought the Bentley to a halt in the vast forecourt of Valeo Hall.

The breath caught in Roxy's throat as she looked up at the enormous golden building. 'Oh...wow!'

'Like it?' he questioned, with silky pride.

'*Like* it?' There was a pause as she allowed herself to drink in the beauty of the place. 'Oh, Titus—it's *amazing*!'

Two bronze lions stood guard, their jaws locked in silent roar as they stared down from two enormous plinths. Giant pillars lined the wide steps leading up to the main door, where an attractive woman in her thirties was standing waiting for them.

Her dark hair was woven neatly on top of her head and she was wearing an elegant grey dress, which was clearly some kind of uniform.

'Come and meet Vanessa,' said Titus.

Shrugging on her warm jacket, Roxy got out of the car—hanging back a little as Titus walked towards the steps.

'How lovely to see you, Your Grace!' said the woman, in a soft voice. 'Did you have a good journey?'

'Very good thanks, Vanessa,' Titus answered. 'The roads were surprisingly quiet.'

Roxy blinked. Your *Grace*? Surely people didn't still say that kind of thing? But Titus was gesturing towards her—looking a bit like a man who was trying to pass off a secondhand car as roadworthy.

'This is Roxanne,' he was saying to the housekeeper. 'You remember me telling you about her on the phone? She's a qualified cleaner, but don't forget she's been ill—so do break her in gently, won't you?'

'Of course I will,' said Vanessa, giving Roxy a cautious smile. 'Welcome to Valeo, Roxanne. We're all pretty busy with the arrangements for His Grace's party—so I can certainly find plenty for you to do here!'

Roxy nodded, unable to shake off a sudden feeling of deflation. She was going to miss the company of Titus, she realised—even though he'd just described her as a 'qualified cleaner'. Her time of being alone with him had come to an end and now she was going to have to blend in and get on with it, just like everyone else. She forced an answering smile. 'Thank you. I'm…I'm really looking forward to working here.'

'Good. Well, I'll show you around now, so that we can leave His Grace in peace,' said Vanessa. 'I'm afraid it will take you ages before you start to find your bearings—it *is* rather a large house.'

'So I see,' said Roxy. She looked up to find a pair of pewter eyes studying her and she felt the unsteady lurch of her heart as she returned his gaze with a polite smile. 'Thanks very much for the lift, Your…er… Your Grace.'

'The pleasure was all mine,' he answered coolly.

He turned and walked into the big house

and Roxy stood there for a moment, feeling a bit like a child who had just lost her security blanket, until Vanessa's voice broke into her thoughts.

'Come inside,' said the housekeeper.

Roxy had thought that entering Valeo Hall was going to be a bit like booking into a smart hotel, but all thoughts of hotels faded the moment she stepped inside. A vast, marbled staircase led up to the first floor and was supported by huge alabaster columns—so that it felt a bit like standing in the British Museum, on a school trip. Looking up, she could see high, domed ceilings with carved and gilded cornices. Exquisite tapestries hung from dark wooden walls and chandeliers like complicated cascades of diamonds sent fractured rays of light across the expanse of floor.

But it was the scale of the place which was so startling. Everything looked so vast that it made her perception seem warped. A chair sitting by the start of the staircase—presumably in case you got exhausted after the long walk across the hall—looked as tiny as a piece of furniture from a doll's house.

'Good heavens,' said Roxy, underneath her breath—but Vanessa must have heard her because she smiled.

'I know. It's pretty amazing the first time you see it, isn't it? I remember walking in here for the first time and not quite believing I was going to be allowed to stay!' She fixed Roxy with a curious look. 'I believe you're just here on a short-term contract, until after His Grace's birthday party?'

Roxy nodded. 'That's right,' she said, as something in the formal-sounding terms of her employment reinforced the Duke's inaccessibility 'Is it going to be a big party?'

'About three hundred and fifty guests, I believe.'

'Gosh,' Roxy observed wryly. 'He must have a lot of friends.'

There was a split-second pause. *'He?'* echoed Vanessa, with a slightly studied expression of surprise. 'The Duke's friendships are not really any of my business— and neither are they yours. I'm afraid that you'll be much too busy polishing all the glassware and dusting the statues to spend time thinking about His Grace's private life! And now, I'll take you across to your room if you like.'

Roxy felt an unexpected twist of disappointment. 'You mean I'm not staying here?'

Vanessa's head jerked back, as if Roxy had committed her second faux pas in as many minutes. 'In the main house? Good heavens, no. Did you think you might be? The workers' cottages are about a five-minute walk away, over by the windmill. As staff accommodation goes, you'll find it's excellent and I'm sure you'll be perfectly comfortable there. Just let me get my coat and I'll take you—it's pretty wintry outside.'

It certainly was, thought Roxy as an icy wind greeted them and chilled her through to the bone. The clouds were dark and heavy but it seemed almost too cold to snow. They crunched their way across the frosty grass until they'd reached a row of small cottages and when Vanessa unlocked the door of one, it was so low that Roxy had to dip her head to enter.

Inside it was simply furnished and compact, with tiny windows looking out onto the flat Norfolk landscape. There was a green furry crocodile lying on the sofa and a used mug on the coffee table, next to a half-eaten packet of digestive biscuits. Vanessa gave a little click of disapproval.

'You'll be sharing with Amy—one of our permanent cleaners, who's about your age.'

'Sharing?' echoed Roxy, because the last time she'd shared had been when The Lollipops were starting out and they'd been jammed into dingy little digs and had nearly killed each other.

'His Grace didn't mention that? I suppose he didn't realise. You'll have your own bedroom, of course,' added Vanessa crisply. 'I did ask Amy to make sure that the place was tidy before you arrived. I'm sorry about the mess.'

'That's okay,' said Roxy automatically.

'Staff dinner will be in the main house, at six-thirty,' Vanessa was saying. 'And whatever you do, don't be late. We have a brilliant cook but she doesn't take kindly to poor timekeeping. Now, unless you've got any questions, I'll leave you to unpack.'

After the housekeeper had left, Roxy unpacked her suitcase and made herself a cup of tea in the small and very old-fashioned kitchen. Her hands cupping the steaming drink, she walked over to the window and stared out at the darkening sky. And she thought how bizarre fate could sometimes be and the different places it could take you.

She had ended up working in a stately home, in the most subservient position of her life. It wasn't ideal, but it was a lifesaver.

And the last thing she could afford to do was to start falling for her arrogant and aristocratic boss.

CHAPTER FIVE

ROXY had never heard of a 'vermicular collar' or a 'large, conical foot'. But there again, she hadn't realised that you could pay as much for a rare, Georgian wine glass as most people would spend on their monthly rent. Or that she would be expected to polish hundreds of the wretched things during the frantic run-up to the Duke's party.

She sighed as she held another delicate goblet up to the light and watched it sparkle, imagining herself toasting the birthday boy. What would she say to him, if she was speaking from the heart? *Here's to Titus Alexander, the icy-eyed Duke who I can't stop thinking about—or fantasising about, even though I'm obviously the kind of woman he despises.*

'So this is where you've been hiding yourself.'

A familiar aristocratic drawl interrupted her dreamy thoughts and Roxy very nearly dropped the precious glass, her fingers only just clamping around the twisted stem in time to save it. And she turned round to find herself looking into a pair of mocking grey eyes.

It seemed like a year since she'd last spoken to him and yet it was barely a week. A week when she'd resolutely gone about her work and tried to forget about her charismatic employer and to concentrate on her job. But Titus's presence seemed to permeate every aspect of his stately home. Everything revolved around the Duke and the Duke's wishes.

Occasionally, she'd seen him striding around the house but she'd spoken to him only once, when the housekeeper had asked her to take two glasses of whisky along to the Morning Room. Roxy had found Titus sitting talking to his estate manager and he had glanced up when she'd walked in and said, 'Ah, Roxanne,' in a way which had made his companion give him a sharp look. Her hands had been trembling as she'd put the tray down and when she had straightened up it had been to find his eyes fixed very firmly on her legs...

Her hands were trembling now as she put the wine glass down and tried to compose her face into a nonchalant expression, but it wasn't easy. Not when he was wearing an outrageously close-fitting pair of jodhpurs, which clung like syrup to his narrow hips and taut thighs.

Roxy looked up into his smoky grey eyes and felt an instant kick of lust. 'Yes, here I am,' she said lightly.

'Had any breakages yet?' His sardonic gaze travelled towards the glass, which was now sitting safely on the table.

'I'm afraid I dropped two just this morning,' she answered blithely and saw his face go slightly pale.

'You're kidding?'

'Funnily enough, yes, I am. I might be getting dazed from staring at so much Georgian crystal, but so far—I've managed to keep them all intact.'

'Good.' There was a pause while he tried not to stare at the soft curve of her lips. Or stop to ask himself why he had deliberately come looking for her after vowing that he would continue to stay away. Perhaps because she had been haunting his nights with the kind of hot and erotic dreams which were usually the province of sexually frustrated teenage boys. And that was crazy when there was an instant solution to his dilemma, if dilemma it was. He could pick up the phone and have someone here by the end of the afternoon, if he wanted to. There were legions of women—beautiful women of his own class—who would have been overjoyed to receive such a summons from the Duke of Torchester.

Yet wasn't it frustrating to realise that currently there was nobody who turned him on the way that Roxy Carmichael did? He was obsessed by her—or, rather, by the thought of having sex with her—and was wondering whether it was worth fighting a battle with himself any longer. Because it was pretty clear from the darkening of her beautiful blue eyes that the feeling was

mutual, so why not give into the powerful chemistry which was sizzling between
them? Yes, she was a servant and he had
vowed that he wasn't ever going to stray
into that rather dangerous territory again,
but sometimes temptation was a little too
much for a man to resist...

He swallowed as he noticed that the but-
tons of her uniform were gaping slightly
to accommodate the luscious swell of her
breasts. 'You've...settled in, I hope?'

'Yes.' Roxy gave a polite little smile.
'Thank you.'

With an effort, Titus forced himself to
ask the type of questions which any employer would ask of his workers—rather
than the ones which were hovering on the
edge of his lips. He wanted to ask if she
realised that he'd seen her yesterday and
she'd been on her knees, scrubbing away
at a spot of something on the floor in the
long corridor of the south wing. And that
the garish pink uniform had been stretched
tightly over her bottom and it had been as
much as he could do not to go over there
and...and...

'And do you like working here?' he enquired unevenly.

Roxy tried not to squirm beneath his smouldering gaze, but it was proving pretty tough. When he was looking at her like that, she wanted to put down her specialist dusting cloth and go over and curl her fingers around his neck. She wanted to stand on tiptoe and to kiss him. And she wanted a lot more besides. She wondered what that virile body would feel like if it was pressing against her. How it would feel to have Titus Alexander take her into his arms and shower her with kisses...

Oh, for heaven's sake! Get *real, Roxy!* Furiously, she made the image dissolve. *He's paying you to do a mundane job and you're here because he feels some lingering sense of responsibility towards you. He hasn't got a glass slipper hidden in his back pocket, so forget your foolish fantasies. You might want him and he might want you— but having sex with the Duke of Torchester would be the worst thing you could possibly do. So stop flirting.*

'It's okay,' she said, thinking that a touch of indifference might drive him away.

Titus scowled, because surely that attitude of hers was another indicator of her general unsuitability to be his lover. Even if it wasn't exactly her dream job—surely she could have been gracious enough to make some comment about the beauty of his ancestral home. Not to shrug her shoulders as if he were forcing her to work in some sort of hovel. A spark of familial pride made him suck in a breath of quiet displeasure. 'You show remarkably little enthusiasm for one of the finest houses in England,' he remarked.

'Maybe that's because I haven't really seen much of its finery—I've been too busy working.'

'Perhaps you might like to go upstairs and polish these glasses in the Grand Saloon?' he questioned sarcastically.

She met his eyes. 'I might.'

Titus felt his lips quirking into a reluctant smile as she looked at him with that mutinous expression on her face as if she were the Queen of Sheba! Did she have any idea how *outrageous* her behaviour was? Maybe she thought that her one-time fame entitled her to certain concessions and that a different set of rules would apply to her. Or maybe she still thought of herself as some kind of goddess—even though today her hair was pulled back into a rather unforgiving ponytail and she wore very little make-up. Still, nobody could deny her inherent grace as she lifted her chin in a defiant tilt, which showcased her long neck. And the way she was staring up at him from between her lashes was making her blue eyes look curiously innocent.

But she wasn't innocent, he reminded himself grimly. He knew that, even if her sexual history hadn't been so well documented in the press. She had shown herself capable of using men—stupid men like Martin Murray. Even if she hadn't actually slept with him, she had still manipulated him to get herself a cheap place to live. And Titus didn't *trust* women like that. He didn't *like* women like that.

If only he could get her out of his head! Or work out what it was about her which had so captured his imagination. The thought of her had been plaguing the hell out of him for days now, even though he'd done his best to keep his distance.

Yet inevitably, he'd seen her around. He had walked past the Statue Gallery the other day when she'd been busy dusting the bust of one of his ancestors—a rather ruthless army general, with a reputation for having been a legendary lover. She'd been oblivious to his presence, and Titus had watched Roxanne run her finger down over the marble cheekbones, to linger at last on the statue's mouth, tracing the line of the cold lips as if they were made of flesh and blood. And for one highly charged moment he had imagined her touching *his* lips like that.

Another time, he had watched her walking from her cottage over to the great house from the high vantage point of his horse's saddle. He had seen the way that the winter wind had whipped through her ponytail, so that it had streamed behind her like a pale, silken banner. She had moved with a natural grace—all the more remarkable because, once again, she had been completely unaware that he'd been watching her. For one heady and insane moment, he had imagined galloping towards her and hauling her up onto the saddle and then taking her away for an afternoon of pure bliss. But he hadn't slept with a servant since he'd been a teenager and he had vowed never to repeat it after the ensuing uproar. The serving classes were too emotional, he had decided. They mistook lust for love. Or, rather, they used the word *love* to justify their lust. Titus felt his lips harden into a mirthless smile. Why couldn't they just be honest and admit there was no such thing?

He noticed that she had now rather self-consciously resumed her glass polishing, even though the stiff set of her shoulders indicated that she was still sensitive to his presence. Would it hurt to be alone with her for a while? he wondered. To give into a desire which it seemed almost criminal to deny? Especially as she was no blushing innocent. Why, she was probably as sexually experienced as he was!

'Would you like me to show you the

house?' he questioned carelessly. 'I mean, properly.'

Roxy looked up from her polishing and raised her eyebrows. 'As opposed to improperly?'

'That could also be arranged,' he drawled.

Roxy quickly put the glass down. 'You mean like an official guided tour?'

'If you like.' His mouth hardened as he caught the glint of sensuality in her smile. 'The only thing is that I'm afraid I don't have a uniform.'

'That's a shame.' She looked at him, knowing that this was highly unprofessional behaviour on both their parts and yet somehow unable to stop herself. Because she was fast discovering that flirting was a bit like riding a bicycle and that you never forgot how to do it, no matter how long it had been. 'I like a man in uniform.'

Her voice dipped suggestively and he very nearly caught her to him then. Only the thought that someone might come in stopped him and he cursed the sudden jerk of an erection. 'On second thoughts, the uniform might have to wait,' he said unevenly, wondering whether the hardening at his groin in the unforgiving jodhpurs was as noticeable to her as it was to him. He pointed to her polishing cloth. 'Leave that and come with me.'

'Vanessa told me to finish it.'

'I'll deal with Vanessa. You can finish it later. Don't you know that the Duke's desires outweigh all other considerations, Roxanne?'

He said it as if he were joking, but Roxy didn't think he *was* joking. Suddenly, there was a very different tension about him and the glint in his eyes hinted at the very real possibility of pleasure. Roxy wondered if she was getting out of her depth and how he'd react if she told him that she answered to the housekeeper and not to him. But she said no such thing. She just put her cloth down and began to follow him from the room, her heart thumping like crazy.

'First,' he said as they walked through to an enormous room which led off the great hall, 'we have what is known as the Grand Saloon.'

Roxy followed him into the massive

space which was decorated in dark crimson and gilded with gold-leaf. 'Well, nobody could accuse it of not living up to its name,' she said. Lightly, she touched the arm of a chair covered in rich, embossed velvet, her fingertips sinking into the soft pile. 'This is beautiful velvet.'

'It comes from Genoa,' he said.

'Where else?' she murmured as she wandered around the room, wondering how long it had taken to build a place like this or to furnish it so beautifully.

'Come and see the Drawing Room now. You'll find that's a much more accessible size.'

'I think we might have differing ideas on accessibility, Titus.'

As they moved from the Saloon Titus cursed himself for using such a provocative word. One which was making him think of the body beneath the garish pink overall she was wearing. Even the bizarre realisation that she shouldn't really be using his Christian name during working hours was driven clean from his mind by the hot clamour of sexual urgency. 'You might be right,' he said thickly.

After she had admired the slightly smaller Drawing Room, he took her into the Picture Gallery, where sumptuous paintings hung in rows along the wood-panelled walls. This was one room she hadn't yet been allowed to work in—she knew that some of the works were price-less and Vanessa had got her on some kind of probationary period to see if she could be trusted. It was as impressive as any gov-ernment art gallery she'd ever visited and for a moment Roxanne was so overcome by the beauty of the paintings that she said nothing.

She knew that he was watching her as they walked slowly along the row of pic-tures and she *liked* him watching her, even though it was making her breasts tingle with excitement. She stopped in front of a painting of a naked woman who was brush-ing her hair, and gave a little sigh.

'You like that one?' he questioned idly.

'It's my favourite. It's *gorgeous*. She looks so fleshy and so *real*—you almost feel you could reach out and pinch her. Though obviously, I'm not going to do that,' she added hastily.

He gave a faint smile. 'Obviously.'

They moved along to the next painting but by now Roxy was beginning to feel uncomfortable—as if the silence which was building between them was somehow becoming dangerous. That if she didn't break it soon, she might blurt out something completely inappropriate—like would he please just kiss her. Maybe she should seek refuge in a bit of small talk. He must be good at that.

She cleared her throat. 'So what exactly does a Duke do all day?'

'No ideas?' he questioned as he watched her peer at a huge canvas of a battle scene.

'Some.' Roxy straightened up to look at him, thinking that his face was infinitely more pleasurable than looking at a load of men wielding swords. 'I know you start the day by going out for a ride, because I've heard the grooms grumbling that you're usually up at the crack of dawn.'

'They sometimes grumble to me, as well,' he conceded.

'And then someone serves you breakfast. I know that because I've seen the cook fussing over your poached eggs and saying that "His Grace likes his toast *just* so".'

Her mimicry was so uncannily accurate that Titus had to bite back a reluctant smile, for fear that he might be encouraging some sort of domestic insubordination. 'And after breakfast?'

Roxy was momentarily distracted by eyes which were as brooding as a gathering storm and wondered if he had any idea how fast her heart was beating. 'You disappear into your study for most of the morning.'

'And what do you think I do there?' he questioned.

She shrugged. 'Oh, I don't know. Play Angry Birds on your computer?'

'I've never found mindless computer games a particularly good use of my time,' he responded acidly.

'Maybe you make a few phone calls before lunch?'

The look he threw her was cool and assessing. 'So, essentially, what you're saying is that you think my days are composed of indulgence and eating?'

Roxy's skin grew heated—but what woman *wouldn't* get all hot and bothered if Titus Alexander was staring at them like that? And maybe he had a point. He didn't look a bit like a man who spent his life being indulgent—in fact, he looked more like someone who did hard, physical labour from dawn to dusk.

'I guess that was a pretty poor assessment,' she said slowly.

'I think perhaps it was. Maybe I should enlighten you by telling you how I've spent my days recently, Roxanne.' His gaze was steady but his breathing was not, as he realised exactly what he was about to do. 'You see, contrary to what the grooms say, I've actually been waking later than usual.'

'Oh, dear. Perhaps your alarm clock needs replacing?'

'I don't usually need an alarm clock. But then I don't usually spend my nights tossing and turning and being unable to get one thing out of my mind.'

'It's true what they say,' she said seriously. 'That the more you think about not being able to sleep, the more elusive it becomes.'

'I'm not talking about my damned sleep!'

'I'm sorry, Titus—but you most definitely were.'

Frustrated by the verbal games they seemed to be playing, he reached out and caught hold of her. He pulled her right up against him and gazed down into her widened blue eyes, feeling the hard heat at his groin and the unsteady thunder of his heart. 'I'm talking about *you*,' he grated. 'Yes, you. Because I can't seem to get you out of my head, Roxanne—no matter what I do.'

His eyes were blazing and Roxy's mouth dried as she felt the heat of his body next to hers. 'But I thought I wasn't your type,' she objected. 'And you're definitely not mine.'

He gave a hard smile. 'Are you sure about that?'

'Quite sure.'

'Liar,' he said softly, and kissed her.

It was like putting a match to dry tinder—more instant and predictable than anything she could ever have anticipated. Roxy's lips opened like a clam as he slid his tongue inside her mouth and snaked his hands possessively around her waist. And suddenly he was kissing her as she'd never been kissed before. Through the powerful burst of pleasure, Roxy felt momentarily dazed. It felt like the lyrics to all those songs Justina had written, the ones Roxy used to sing without really believing. The ones about bells ringing and angels singing and feeling as if you'd just stepped onto a merry-go-round which was going so fast you that wondered if you'd ever get off again. But who would want to get off something which felt as incredible as *this*? Who wouldn't want to prolong each precious, glorious second?

His hands began to skate down over her body. She could feel his fingers splaying hungrily over her breasts. She was conscious of the tight thrust of her nipples as they strained against her pink overall and she moaned against his mouth.

Titus heard her breathy little gasp and suddenly he forgot where he was or who he was. He forgot his timetable and plans for the day. All he could think about was Roxanne Carmichael and the tantalising prospect of having quick and urgent sex with her. Savagely, he snapped open the poppers of her pink overall, slipping his hand underneath her sweater to feel the puckering nipple beneath her bra. He pictured it in all its cherry-tipped glory and felt her wild shudder in response to the flick of his thumb over the peaking mound.

'Roxanne,' he shuddered.

'Titus.' She said his name like a plea, especially as he had just moved his hand down and was sliding it up beneath her uniform. Up her legs, and over her thighs and…

'I want you,' he ground out as his hand cupped the moist panty-covered core of her femininity. 'I don't want to wait a second longer. I already feel like I've been waiting an eternity to do this. I want to lay you right down there on that rug and to unzip myself and to—'

She sensed rather than heard the profanity which was hovering on his lips and which was halted by the distant sound of footsteps clacking their way towards them. For a moment they both froze, before Roxy pushed his hand away from her knickers and shrank away from him in horror.

'It's Vanessa!' she hissed, tugging down her sweater and swiftly doing up her over-all.

'Stay there,' he instructed curtly, pain-fully aware of the erotic scent of her sex which had permeated the air around them. 'Don't go anywhere.'

Where else did he think she was going to go? Rush up to greet the housekeeper with her uniform gaping open and her sweater all rucked up, her movements slightly jerky and awkward because she was so aroused? She thought how composed he looked as he ran his fingers through his thick, tawny hair and began to walk towards the en-trance to the gallery. She could see the housekeeper approaching, with a rather odd smile pinned to her lips.

'Your Grace,' she said formally.

'Ah, Vanessa,' he said imperturbably. 'I do hope I haven't interfered with your schedule—but it was Roxanne's lunch break and I'd promised that I'd show her the paintings.' He glanced over at the picture of the woman standing in front of the mirror and then slanted Roxy a conspiratorial look, a faint smile curving his lips as he took in her flushed cheeks and bright eyes. 'She seems to have taken rather a shine to the Rubens.'

'Does she now?' said Vanessa and Roxy wondered if she was imagining the *knowing* look on the housekeeper's face.

'So I think perhaps we might leave her in peace to study it, don't you?'

He spoke in the kind of tone which nobody would dare question, least of all his housekeeper, but as he turned to leave he gave Roxy a faintly condescending nod. The type of farewell which a Duke would normally be expected to give to his most junior of servants. And she wondered if her face betrayed the guilt which was churning away inside her. Or the frustration.

'Oh, look,' he said, to no one in particular, his attention drawn to the enormous windows. 'It's started snowing.'

CHAPTER SIX

THE wind whipped up the snow like cream in a food processor and Roxy hugged her jacket closer as she stumbled through the fierce afternoon weather towards her cottage. The change to the flat Norfolk landscape had been dramatic since the storm had begun. Big, fat flakes had been tumbling incessantly from the sky and a few hours had seen enough snow falling to turn the estate into a winter wonderland. The wide parkland was now bleached white and Valeo Hall looked indescribably beautiful, with thick blankets of snow on every roof and chimney pot.

The older staff had moaned about the extra work but Roxy had been *glad* of nature's intervention. Glad that the wintry transformation had distracted her from the infinitely more disturbing memory of what had happened in the picture gallery at lunch-time.

Despite the icy weather, she could feel her cheeks burning as she let herself into her cottage. She quickly shut the door on the inclement weather and could see from the lit fire and biscuit crumbs that Amy was at home.

'Hello?' she called loudly.

There was a thump from upstairs and then an answering voice. 'I'm in the *bath*!'

Roxy was pleased not to have to face her housemate. She felt so shaken by her encounter with Titus that she wasn't sure she'd be able to have a coherent conversation with anyone—let alone the bubbly Amy who still couldn't quite believe she was sharing a cottage with an ex-member of The Lollipops.

Shaking the snow from her jacket and pulling off her boots, Roxy walked over to the fire and stood with her palms splayed out in front of the dancing flames.

Was she *insane*—to have been so eager and responsive when her aristocratic boss had seduced her? She grimaced. Not that he'd needed to do much actual seducing. She had launched herself into his arms like a heat-seeking missile and if Vanessa hadn't suddenly appeared, she wondered if she would have let him do what he said he wanted to do.

Lay her right down there on that carpet and—

She felt the tension in her body as she remembered the harsh way he had bitten out those words. Yet she could hardly blame him for being so graphic when she'd been leading him on. Making those flippant little comments and smiling those knowing little smiles. But when he'd started kissing her…something had changed. It had stopped being a game and it had felt deadly serious. She'd gone up in flames—as if he'd put some kind of spell on her. She tried telling herself that it was because it had been so long since she'd made love that she'd responded to him so passionately. Wasn't that an infinitely preferable reason for her behaviour? Because the alternative was that

Titus Alexander had liberated emotions which up until now had been locked away.

A fierce pounding on the front door startled her, but not nearly as much as the muffled sound of an imperious voice.

'Open the bloody door!'

Heart racing, she pulled open the door and was almost knocked over by the fierce wind which gusted in. A tall figure, covered in white, stepped inside and despite her confused thoughts, Roxy started laughing.

'What's so funny?' growled Titus as he shook the thick layer of snow from his dark overcoat.

'You look like a snowman!'

'And right now I feel like one. For God's sake, let me in.'

'You can't come in!' she muttered.

'What do you mean, I can't come in? I can do any damned thing I please.' He walked straight past her and thrust a bottle of wine into her hand. 'I come bearing gifts—so why don't you go and open this, like a good girl?'

Roxy's fingers automatically closed around

the bottle but his breathtaking arrogance combined with somebody calling her a 'good girl' was enough to tempt her into telling him just what he could do with his wine. But her thoughts were far more focused on the very real fear that Amy would come bouncing downstairs at any moment, clad only in a towel.

She put the bottle of wine down on the dresser and turned to him. 'Titus, I mean it. You can't—'

'It's too late for that,' he said savagely and pulled her into his arms to kiss her.

It was a hungry, almost brutal kiss which instantly drove all thoughts of Amy clean out of Roxy's mind. It obliterated everything but the desire to have more. His face was icy but his lips were warm and she could feel snowflakes melting on her cheeks as they fell from his tawny hair. Unsteadily, she reached up to grip the broad lines of his shoulders, her fingers kneading luxuriously against their powerful musculature.

'Titus,' she breathed. 'This is insane.'

'Now that,' he agreed unsteadily, 'I would

agree with. But you know something? It just feels too good to stop.'

His mouth came down on hers again, blotting out all her doubts and uncertainties. His hands moulded the shape of her body and now he was moving one of them down towards her belly and was rucking up her skirt. She could feel the grazing urgency of his fingers as they moved over her thigh and she moaned as they slipped aside the panel of her knickers to delve into her molten heat. 'Oh, God, Titus. You can't—'

'Can't I?' His breath felt warm against her cheek, his heart pounding so ferociously that he thought it might explode. 'Don't you like that?'

'You know I do,' she gasped.

'Well, so do I.' His breathing was laboured; he felt more excited than he'd felt in a long time—perhaps ever. He wanted to *devour* her. To taste and touch every delicious inch of her. Luxuriously, he strummed his finger against her aroused flesh, wanting her compliant and gasping in his arms before he carried her upstairs to bed.

'T-Titus.'

'Shh.' He silenced her with another kiss, hearing the urgent little moans she made in time with her rising breath. He was luxuriating in the sticky, sensual feel of her until he became vaguely aware of a distant sound and he wrenched his lips away from hers, though his finger kept moving. 'What's that noise?'

'My…my housemate,' she managed to gasp.

'Your *housemate*?' he echoed furiously.

'Y-yes. She's…she's in the bath!'

Furiously, he snatched his hand free and took a step away from her intoxicating proximity. 'This is fast becoming a farce,' he hissed.

Despite her own deep sense of frustration, Roxy couldn't resist the hint of a smile. Because suddenly, with that dark, truculent expression on his face and his sensual lips forming a decided pout, she could see *exactly* what he must have looked like as a little boy.

'Titus not getting what he wants?' she teased as she struggled to get her breath back.

His eyes met hers. 'I'd say it was more a case of Roxanne not getting what *she* wants, wouldn't you?' he murmured as his gaze flicked deliberately over her heaving breasts. 'Does she go out? Your house-mate?'

Roxy nodded, that brazenly sexual scrutiny of his making it difficult for her to get any words out. 'Y-yes. In fact, she's getting ready to go out now. She works in the village pub some evenings.'

'What time?'

'She leaves here at seven. Titus, you must go. Please. Unless you want her to come downstairs and find you.'

For a moment, Titus reflected on the irony of being shown out of one of his own properties by this most junior member of his staff. And the sight of her ruffled hair and flushed cheeks was enough to tempt his best resolve. Couldn't he just take her upstairs and lock the door—and to hell with the housemate? Surely she didn't have to share a *bedroom*? But sanity prevailed as with an almighty effort he walked over to the door.

'I'll be back,' he promised on a silken whisper as he pulled the door open and went out into the blizzard.

Roxy was trembling when she shut the door behind him and she ran upstairs to her tiny bedroom, unwilling to face Amy when she was still in such a state. She leaned on the dressing table to support herself and closed her eyes, overcome by a combination of guilt and pleasure.

Had that really just happened? Had Titus Alexander just come to her house and almost brought her to orgasm, while she had clung to him like a wild woman and almost *let* him?

She glanced at her watch as she heard Amy leave the bathroom and then begin to move around in her bedroom next door. It was now gone six and Titus had said he was coming back at seven. The question was whether she geared herself up to telling him that it was a big mistake and that she'd changed her mind. Because wouldn't that be the most sensible thing to do? For both of them.

She felt the rapid beat of her heart, know-

ing that she wouldn't. She *couldn't*. She
didn't want her enduring memory of Titus
to be some furtive little encounter on the
doorstep of one of his properties. Didn't
it feel like for ever since she'd felt passion
like this? She wanted to make love with
him properly and with no holds barred. She
wanted to hold him in her arms afterwards
and to cradle his tawny head until he fell
asleep. She wanted to kiss his skin and to
breathe in his own, very particular scent.

Walking into the still steam-filled bathroom, she turned on the bath. She would
pull out all the stops before he got here, and
then, then—

'Roxy!'

Above the spluttering gurgle of the hot
tap, Roxy lifted her head to hear Amy's
shout. 'What?'

'Can you come here for a second?'

For a moment Roxy felt a pang of genuine panic, as if she'd left some incriminat-
ing piece of evidence to show what had just
taken place.

With reluctant steps she went downstairs to see Amy wrapping a chiffon scarf

around her neck, prior to leaving for her part-time job at the local pub. She often complained that the Torchester estate didn't pay her nearly enough, though Roxy suspected that the pub work had more to do with the male eye-candy regularly seen propping up the bar.

She and Amy had hit it off immediately—though Amy's friendly attitude had been tinged with disbelief when she'd recognised Roxy as having been a member of The Lollipops.

This happened less and less—in fact, it hardly happened at all, these days. Roxy wondered if it was because she was getting too old to be associated with a girl-band, or maybe her undyed hair and minimal make-up was super efficient as a disguise. Roxy didn't mind. At least not being recognised meant you didn't have to endure all those questions which always began with, 'Didn't you *used* to be…?' and ended up by making her feel a failure.

But Amy had been a genuine fan of the band—she'd bought *Sweet and Sticky*, which had been The Lollipops' first album.

She'd even been to one of their concerts—
the one where Justina had famously been
wearing the sequined hot pants. Her genuine liking of the band's music had made
Roxy feel a rare pang of nostalgia for her
crazy days on tour with the group.

Amy gave the chiffon scarf a final twist
and pointed at the dresser. 'What's that?'

'What?' questioned Roxy, still feeling
slightly dazed by Titus's provocative visit.

'This!' Amy picked up the bottle of wine
and glanced down at the label. 'Chateau
Margaux,' she read, before looking up to
give Roxy a questioning look. 'Now, I'm
no wine buff but even I know that this isn't
your average plonk. Where did you get it?'

'I…' Roxy sucked in a deep breath. 'Titus
gave it to me.'

'Titus?'

'Um, I mean—the Duke.'

Amy's brows did another swift elevation.
'The Duke gave you a bottle of expensive
wine?'

Roxy nodded. 'Yes, he did. Because…
because I managed to catch one of his expensive Georgian glasses before it tumbled

to the ground. Did you realise that those glasses cost over six hundred quid?'

'No, I didn't,' said Amy slowly.

'So I did him a big favour, really. Saved him a lot of money.' Roxy flashed a smile as she consoled herself with the thought that it was the truth—or at least a variation of the truth. No need to tell her housemate that the glass wouldn't have been in danger if the Duke himself hadn't walked into the room and made her fingers tremble so much that she'd almost dropped it. 'Gotta run,' she breathed. 'Mustn't let my bath overflow!'

Roxy ran back upstairs to the tiny bathroom just in time to stop water from slopping over the sides, and she had to let the plug out for a minute before she risked getting in. Her bath was rapid rather than relaxing and afterwards she pulled on a long, crushed velvet skirt and teamed it with a beautiful cashmere sweater she'd had for ages, but which she hardly ever wore because she wanted to preserve it. She brushed her hair and applied lip-gloss and perfume—but it wasn't until she heard Amy leaving that she risked going downstairs and she flinched as she caught sight of herself in the hall mirror.

She looked...

She swallowed.

She couldn't ever remember looking quite so *shiny* before. Her eyes were glittering wildly and her lips glimmered with their shimmering of gloss. Her dark-blonde hair hung in a silky-satin curtain over her shoulders and the combination of cashmere and velvet made her look...*expensive*. As if she'd made an effort. Well, she *had* made an effort.

But the realisation of how much was riding on this made her hesitate as she wondered if she was in danger of becoming some kind of laughing stock. She had spruced herself up for the Duke after that shocking demonstration of how quickly he could turn her on. She was making it very clear that she was a very willing participant in all this—and surely that was the wrong message to send out, particularly to a man like him. Yet it didn't seem that she had an alternative, not when she wanted him so badly.

The minute hand on the clock ticked by so slowly and she started wondering if perhaps the battery was running out. She resisted the urge to go and peep from behind the curtains but by ten past seven, she was climbing the walls with frustration and embarrassment.

He wasn't coming.

It was the worst case of all scenarios.

He had decided that this was a big mistake and best forgotten.

So how on earth would she face him next time she saw him?

But just after she'd pulled the cork on the wine, having decided to drink at least half the contents of the bottle as some kind of miserable compensation, there was a loud banging on the door.

And all thoughts of what she should or shouldn't say were forgotten as she opened the door and fell into his arms.

His kiss was heated and urgent, his embrace hard and possessive. Roxy made a distracted little sound as Titus moved away from her, shutting the door on the snowy night. And then he came back and tangled his fingers in her hair, his eyes narrowed as he looked down at her eager face for a moment before asking coolly, 'I'm assuming she's gone?'

Roxy nodded.

He pushed her up against the wall and then pressed his body up against hers in a very deliberate display of masculine mastery. She could feel the proud jut of his hips and the steely shaft of his erection as it nudged against her and she drew in a deep breath of excitement mingled with a stupid kind of nervousness.

'Do you know how slowly these last two hours have passed?' he questioned unsteadily as he pulled her sweater out from the waistband of her velvet skirt.

'I th-think I have a good idea,' she breathed.

His fingers were brushing against her bare skin and he was murmuring little sounds of appreciation into her ear and instantly Roxy felt the melting response of her hungry body. And suddenly she was afraid it was all going to happen too quickly, the way it had done before. That it would be the perfunctory pursuit of pleasure and then he might leave—and she wouldn't get a chance to savour this magnificent man. Perhaps he read her thoughts—or maybe it suited her to think that—because he lifted his head and his grey eyes narrowed in question.

'Are you going to take me upstairs?' he whispered, his finger finding her belly button and kneading at it with erotic thoroughness. 'Or are you angling to have me do it to you right here, up against the wall?'

'No,' she whispered back. 'Come…come with me.' She turned and headed for the staircase, acutely aware of him behind her—her heart pounding as she led him into her room. Briefly, she saw him glance round in surprise and she thought that the fairly featureless little bedroom must look so very different from his own, back in the great house.

Outside, their lives were so different, she thought. But in this anonymous little room, those differences didn't matter. He might be a Duke and she might be a singer who'd fallen on hard times, but in this one very fundamental act, at least, they were equals.

'Is this better?' she questioned as she went into his waiting arms.

'Much. And this is better still.' His mouth brushed over hers with featherlight tease. 'Don't you think?'

'Yes,' she whispered but the unexpected tenderness was tantalising. He began to kiss her again and suddenly Roxy understood why women sometimes said it made them feel faint when a man kissed them. She felt like that now. As if she might have slid to the ground in some helpless kind of swoon if Titus hadn't been holding her. And that feeling was *dangerous*.

But danger was easy to ignore—especially when he was undressing her in a way which was making her body shudder. Her velvet skirt whispered to the ground, closely followed by the cashmere sweater. With a smooth dexterity he disposed of her bra and slithered her knickers off, and she found herself revelling in the speculative gleam of his eyes.

'You are very, very beautiful but I think you'd better get into bed,' he instructed shakily. 'You're shivering.'

But Roxy's shivering didn't stop once she was covered by the duvet. If anything it increased, because he had pulled his sweater off and was unzipping his jeans and the slow and complicit way he smiled at her when his erection sprang free actually made her *blush*.

'Oh, Roxanne,' he murmured as he climbed into bed beside her and pulled her into his arms. 'I can't believe you're blushing.'

Neither could she—but there was something about Titus which was making her feel about sixteen. As if this had never happened before. As if the briefest of butterfly touches could start off a whole chain-reaction of feelings which could make her heart clench with wistful longing. And she had better keep those rather pitiful thoughts to herself, she told herself fiercely. Just imagine how much that would inflate his already inflated ego if he knew she could be so instantly smitten.

'Just shut up and kiss me,' she said and he was laughing softly as she pulled his tawny head down towards her.

CHAPTER SEVEN

THE delicate stroking of fingertips over his rib cage roused Titus from the comfortable half-world between waking and sleeping. Slitting open his eyes, he saw from the flickering light which danced shadows around the room that the candle had burned low.

'Titus? Are you awake?'

The voice was soft. Melodic. Like sweet balm on his senses. He gave a lazy yawn before rolling over to survey Roxanne's blue eyes, which were fixed on him, thinking how spectacular she looked in the half-light. Like some kind of wanton goddess. Her fair hair spilled down over her shoulders and her skin was so white it might have been carved from marble. The whiteness was broken by her nipples, which were thrusting towards him in silent invitation.

If he hadn't spent two of the last three hours making love to her, he might have been tempted to lean forward and lick one. Or maybe to kiss her instead. He seemed to have spent an inordinate amount of time kissing her during these snatched and highly erotic interludes at her cottage. He seemed to be walking around his estate in a constant state of arousal. Like a teenager who had just discovered sex. He frowned. Every time he saw her, he wanted to drag her off into the nearest darkened alcove and make love to her—a feat not easily achieved when she was usually wielding a feather duster, with the ever-vigilant Vanessa hovering close by. But sometimes they succeeded, like yesterday—when he had found her alone in the boot-room and he had taken one look at her shining blue eyes and had locked the door.

'Titus? Are you awake?' she repeated.

He yawned again. 'I am now.'

Roxy levered herself up onto her elbow to look at him. Not that there was a lot of room for manoeuvre in this narrow single bed—and certainly not when a man of Titus's stature was sharing it with you.

She drifted her fingertips down over his hard torso, tracing little circles over his flat belly and feeling his hips circle automatically in response. For three weeks now, they'd been lovers and he was the best lover she'd ever had. No, scrub that. Titus seemed like the *only* lover she'd ever had. It was as if she'd come to his bed an innocent and discovered sex through him, and him alone.

How he did that remained something of a mystery—or maybe that was because *he* was still something of a mystery. She knew his body so well. She knew how to reduce him to boneless longing with just the tiptoeing of her fingers—it was getting to know the real man which was harder. No matter how great the intimacy which existed when they were in bed together, he always managed to keep something of himself back. His coolly aristocratic air always seemed to kick in and change the subject, just when it was getting interesting.

She supposed that his reluctance to talk about anything other than the superficial was all to do with his upbringing, because everyone knew that the upper classes didn't 'do' feelings. They kept them buttoned up inside and froze out anyone who dared to enquire. It was just that lately this attitude had begun to frustrate her. She wasn't stupid enough to read anything permanent into what was happening between them— but knowing so little about him sometimes made her feel as if she were in bed with a ghost.

She drew in a deep breath. 'Tell me what it was like, growing up in Scotland.'

Titus narrowed his eyes and he might have been tempted to bat the question away if he hadn't been momentarily distracted by the downward movement of her hand. 'I didn't grow up in Scotland.'

'But you said that your mother lived in Scotland—after your parents divorced. When you were a little boy.'

He swallowed as he felt her fingertips brush against his growing erection. 'And she did. But I stayed here.'

'You stayed here? What, with your father and your *stepmother*?'

'Right again,' he groaned as he felt the trickle of her hand over his aching shaft.

'But I thought you said you hated your stepmother.'

He shot her a dark look as he rolled away from her, reluctant to face an interrogation while her hands were working such sweet magic—because didn't that feel like a kind of *manipulation*? 'We didn't exactly see eye to eye on most subjects, but I don't remember actually using the word *hate*, Roxanne.'

'But that must have been an awful situation,' she continued, even though his grey eyes were flashing out an unmistakable warning. 'You must have missed your mother like mad. And she must have missed you, too.'

He scowled. What a bloody naive thing to say! 'Of course I missed her,' he said. 'But I saw her during some of the school vacations. And anyway, she remarried when I was ten.'

Roxy sensed another big story behind

that flat declaration. 'And do you get on well with your stepfather?'

'A question which is thankfully no longer relevant, since my mother divorced him as well,' he returned caustically. 'My family's track record for holding down a long-term marriage isn't great. Which is probably what makes me view it with as much enthusiasm as I would a trip to the dentist. A necessary duty I'll one day have to undertake in order to secure a suitable succession to the Dukedom.'

She could hear the caustic note underpinning his flippant comment, obviously trying to put her straight about where he stood. The not-very-subtle warning her off about marriage. Well, she certainly wasn't fantasising about herself as the next Duchess—she wasn't that stupid! She just wanted to know him a little better—and why shouldn't she when they were lying naked in bed together? Surely physical intimacy gave you *some* rights?

'Then why didn't you go up to Scotland with her?' she persisted. 'That's what would normally happen. The woman usually gets custody of the child—especially if she's the one who's been "wronged".'

Titus sighed, but more with exasperation than irritation. Didn't she realise that the normal rules simply didn't apply to someone like him? That in his world, the importance of tradition was placed above the close family bonds enjoyed by most people. 'Because I needed to be here. At Valeo. The estate was my inheritance and I needed to learn how to run it—and I could only do that at firsthand. Not living with my mother was considered a necessary sacrifice in order for me to achieve that.'

She reached over to coil her fingers in the thick tawny hair. 'Oh, Titus, that's terrible.'

'No, Roxy, it is not *terrible*. It's just the way things are. My heritage is everything to me. It's what drives me. My duty is what drives me.' He saw the softness in her big blue eyes and something made him want to lash out at her. *Don't look at me that way,* he thought. *Don't make your voice grow all soft and husky with emotion. Don't make me examine things which are best kept locked away.* His voice hardened. 'Why, was your childhood the stuff that dreams are made of?'

Roxy realised that she had walked into a trap of her own making. *She* was usually the one who clammed up when people wanted to know about her upbringing—but she could hardly do that now. Not in light of her own determined line of questioning. She gave a shrug, which didn't quite come off. 'Not unless you dream of having a mother who makes repeated suicide attempts—'

'Oh, God. Roxy, I'm sorry.'

'Why should you be sorry? It isn't your fault.'

He knew from the way she'd screwed up her face that she didn't want to elaborate and normally he would have been only too glad to change the subject, but, inexplicably, he found himself *wanting* to know. Because he had discovered that Roxy was a woman who kept bits of herself locked away—just as he did. And he was discovering that the elusive was curiously tantalising. 'What happened?'

She stared at him, wishing that she'd kept her mouth shut. She was unsuitable enough to be sharing his bed as it was, without admitting to having a mentally unstable mother. But she'd known that all along, hadn't she? She'd known that she was not the kind of woman the Duke would usually be involved with—he had just implied pretty much the same thing himself. So it didn't matter which of her secrets she told him. It would have no effect on their future, because they didn't have a future.

'What happened?' Roxy allowed herself to remember the patchwork of dramatic incidents which had made up her childhood. 'My father's rather *liberated* behaviour was usually what provoked another failed attempt on the part of my mother. She would discover his latest infidelity and there would be an enormous scene. Shouts and screams and plates being hurled—finishing up with a call to the emergency services. It was like living on the set of an opera. The doctors kept saying it was a cry for help— and she certainly never took enough pills to kill herself. I used to go with her to the hospital. She couldn't bear to have my father accompany her because he'd just hurt her again. And more to the point—she hated him seeing her vomiting.' Her gaze was steady. 'I became quite good at giving a concise summary of her medical history.'

He flinched at her deliberate candour— the deadpan look on her face as she recited the facts managing to be much more chilling than a cascade of accompanying emotion. 'So did she kill herself in the end?'

Roxy narrowed her eyes. 'I don't remember telling you that she was dead.'

'You didn't have to.' He shrugged. 'But you speak about her in the past tense.'

Roxy was surprised by his perception. 'Actually, she died in a way which nobody could have anticipated,' she said slowly. 'They were going through one of their kiss-and-make-up phases and she'd gone out to buy a new dress. She was doing that sort of dreamy thing which women do when they think they're loved. She…she wasn't really concentrating on the busy London traffic and she walked straight out in front of a taxi. The end.'

'Oh, God. Roxy.'

'It was a long time ago,' she said fiercely. 'It doesn't hurt any more.' And that much was true. The pain *had* gone away. She'd *made* it go away in order to ensure her own survival, but it had inevitably left behind its own scar tissue. It had been during those fierce attempts to numb the pain that she'd realised it was easier not to let people close. If you didn't let people close, then they couldn't hurt you. Especially men. Up until now, that had never been a problem. She'd never wanted to let anyone close. But now she did. *And Titus Alexander was the worst possible man to have chosen.*

'So it was just you and your father?' he questioned slowly. 'He brought you up?'

'Not really. It was me, my father and whoever his current squeeze was. Until he got bored and dumped her. The women always resented me being around because I cramped their style, although they always pretended to adore me when Dad was watching. But they never lasted long.' She'd seen for herself how badly men could treat women. And how women let themselves be treated badly because they had clung onto some foolish idea of 'love'.

He heard the cynical note which had entered her voice and part of him rejoiced in it. 'So, like me you don't have any illusions about "love"?' he questioned coolly.

Roxy shrugged—because she recognised it as both a question and a warning. 'Of course not,' she said.

'Good.' His eyes gleamed as he took her hand and guided it down to his groin. 'Now, can we please stop talking and do something else?'

She was tempted—oh, how she was tempted. But she was feeling a little bit vulnerable and, more importantly—it was getting late. She pulled her hand away. 'There isn't time. Amy will be back from the pub soon.'

'Damn Amy.'

'That isn't very nice, Titus. She was living here long before I was.' She hesitated and some rogue spark made her say it, even though she knew it was asking for trouble. 'Of course, I could always come and spend the night with you in the great house.'

There was a pause. 'You know we can't do that, Roxy.'

'Well, we *could*,' she argued. 'You're the Duke who can do anything he pleases. You told me that yourself. But clearly you don't want to.'

Didn't he? He studied her blue eyes thoughtfully. Didn't he sometimes wake in the night in his vast four-poster bed and wish that he could reach for her? Hadn't he sometimes thought how blissful mornings might have been if he'd just been able to slide straight into her waiting heat and then run his fingers through the silken tumble of her hair? But protocol made that impossible—as did the thought that Roxanne might read too much into such a gesture.

'If we do that, then we might as well make an announcement to the rest of the staff that we're sleeping together,' he said.

'Actually, sleeping together is one thing we're *not* doing.'

'You know what I mean, Roxanne.'

'Yes, I know exactly what you mean.' The stupid words came tumbling out before she could stop them. 'You're ashamed of me.'

'You're much too smart to come out with something like that,' he said softly. 'I am not ashamed of you—I'm just thinking about your welfare.'

'Ever the solicitous boss!' she mocked.

He tilted her chin up with the tip of his finger. 'Don't you think it might make life awkward for you if people knew that we were involved?'

'You're saying they don't?'

'Why?' He rolled onto his back and studied her from between narrowed eyes. 'Have you been boasting about your encounters with me?'

'Titus Alexander, you are a very arrogant man,' she said crossly. 'I haven't said a word to anyone, but occasionally I wonder if Vanessa has some idea about what's going on. Sometimes I see her looking at me curiously.'

'Oh, Vanessa knows plenty about what goes on in this house,' he said, with a curious smile. 'But *guessing* something is different from being told something. If we were blatant about our liaison then it would undermine her authority—and place you in a potentially awkward situation. It just makes life easier for you this way, that's all. Now, come here and kiss me.'

Easier for *him*, she thought as she shook her head, more from a sense of pride than because she meant it. 'I don't want to kiss you.'

'Don't you?' He reached out and cupped her breast, his thumb circling the hardening nipple. 'Are you quite sure about that, Miss Carmichael?'

Roxy's mouth dried as she felt the urgent stab of sexual hunger. 'You are an outrageous man, Titus.'

'I thought we'd established that a while back.'

'We'll have to be quick,' she whispered.

'Oh, I can be *very* quick.'

She should have resisted, but there was something about Titus which made him impossible to resist. Especially when he was pushing her back against the pillows like that and was moving over her body. She squirmed as he thrust deep inside her, until he awoke the first helpless wave of pleasure. *Oh, Titus,* she thought helplessly as her back began to arch with senseless abandon. *What have you done to me?* She had vowed not to let herself feel too deeply—to keep this affair in its proper place—and yet hadn't she started breaking all those vows as if they'd meant nothing?

It had begun to scare her when she thought about the future, when all this would come to an end. His birthday party was next Saturday and working here permanently had never been in the cards. She knew that. And Titus had never raised false hopes by making promises which he couldn't keep. So hadn't she better be the one to broach leaving, so that at least she'd be able to walk away with her pride intact?

She watched as he began to dress, wishing that the rest of the world didn't exist. That they could stay here, locked in their own private little place. But you couldn't keep a man by locking him up and throwing away the key, could you?

'Was that good?' he murmured as he observed her gaze following him around the room.

She pretended to think about it. 'No, it was absolutely *awful*,' she said. 'But I'm willing to give you another opportunity to get it right, if you play your cards right.'

Titus smiled as he finished buttoning up his shirt. The least educated woman he'd ever met and she also happened to be the smartest. He thought back to all the 'suitable' women who had been trooped out for his approval over the years. He thought about the way they behaved—with all their originality replaced by a breathless acknowledgement of his *eligibility*. And he thought about his imminent birthday party and the aristocratic crumpet who would have their sights set on changing his single status as soon as possible.

He glittered the watchful Roxanne a lazy smile. 'I shall do my very best to improve my technique,' he said.

'Good.' She sat up in bed, determined to break her wistful mood. 'Are you getting excited about your birthday party?'

'Who looks forward to a milestone like thirty-five?'

'Thirty-five isn't old, Titus.'

'Maybe not.' But in ducal terms, Titus knew that it *was.* The pressure was on for him to produce a wife and an heir—and the absence of any brothers had meant that the pressure was mounting. Wasn't there the unspoken fear that, if he didn't hurry up and produce a son, the estate would pass down to some distant cousin who lived in some remote part of Scandinavia?

Duty demanded that he start looking seriously to find a suitable woman to provide him with an heir—and stop wasting his time with Roxanne Carmichael. He watched as she leaned back to pillow her head against her arms. *Foxy Roxy,* the journalists used to call her, describing her as being 'sex on legs' and, looking at her flushed face and naked body, it was easy to see why. *So how the hell could she be suitable for anything other than transitory pleasure?*

He zipped up his jeans. 'I wish I could invite you to the party.'

Roxy shook her head. 'No, you don't. Not really. I'd cramp your style. You'll be expected to dance with all those Honourable Ladies who'll be dazzling you with their diamonds.' And she couldn't bear to watch. Couldn't bear to keep a smile fixed to her face and pretend that she didn't care. Because of course she cared when it had been *her* he'd been making love to—and not some jewel-encrusted fellow aristocrat.

Because that was the trouble with sex, she decided. Especially sex as good as this. It made you feel close to a man, even when you knew that was a bad idea. It made you start having emotions you didn't want to have. A little bit of possessiveness had crept into her heart along the way—and more than a bit of resentment, too. She realised that Titus was hiding her away like a guilty secret and lately she had started to mind.

But there was no point in blowing it, not when this was all destined to come to a natural end very soon.

'And my contract runs out once the party is over,' she said slowly. 'I'll be going back to London.'

Titus nodded as he picked up his sweater, unable to ignore that hopeful little note in her voice. Would it hurt to give her what she so obviously wanted? Some kind of acknowledgement that this hadn't all been about sex. 'Maybe we could go out for a drive or something,' he said vaguely as he glanced at his watch. 'Would you like that?'

It was the closest he'd ever come to asking her out on a date and Roxy nodded, her heart twisting as she registered that he was probably asking her out of some sense of *duty*. She clenched her hands into two little fists, determined that he shouldn't remember her as whining or jealous—as someone who was unable to accept the status quo. She wanted him to remember her as *strong*. When he thought about her in the future, she wanted him to *regret* that she was no longer in his life and not just be glad that she'd gone. 'Sure!' she said brightly. 'That'd be great.'

But after the front door had slammed behind him and she'd quickly blown out the candle so that Amy would think she was asleep, Roxy lay wide-eyed in the darkness.

Realising that she'd talked about leaving and Titus had accepted it as equably as if she'd been talking about the sun rising in the sky every morning.

And that his hard and handsome face hadn't shown a single flicker of regret.

CHAPTER EIGHT

FOUR days later, having first established the time of her afternoon off during a snatched and rather erotic moment in one of the darkened alcoves in the library, Titus took Roxy driving.

'Norfolk is bitingly cold in winter,' he told her sternly. 'So make sure you dress warmly *and* practically.'

Roxy had nodded, quietly jubilant about the fact that for once he was telling her to leave her clothes *on*, instead of being intent on removing them as quickly as possible. Perhaps it was because a statement like that implied a degree of care, rather than simply lust. Or perhaps her ridiculous sense of excitement had something to do with the fact that going out for the afternoon was the kind of thing which *normal* lovers did.

The snow had almost melted and was turning to a thick grey slush. Roxy dressed in jeans and two layers of sweaters, before borrowing a pair of waterproof boots from the boot-room. She tried to keep a sense of perspective about the trip, but her heart was still beating with ridiculous excitement when Titus slowed beside her at their arranged rendezvous at the bottom of the drive.

'I feel like some kind of spy,' she said breathlessly as she climbed into the muddy four-wheel drive. 'As if I'm taking part in some covert operation in case Vanessa finds out what I'm up to.'

Titus drove through the stone arch and out onto the main road. 'And do you mind if she does?'

'Of course I'd mind! I don't want her thinking that I'm the kind of woman who sleeps her way to the top—that I went out of my way to seduce you, when we both know it was the other way round.'

'I don't remember you fighting me very hard, Roxanne.'

'You didn't give me a chance to fight!

And anyway, shouldn't you be worried about *your* reputation?' She shot him a glance as a bottled-up fear came spilling out. 'Unless, of course, this kind of thing happens a lot.'

'This…kind…of…thing?' he repeated.

'Going to bed with someone who works for you.'

His lips hardened into a mocking smile. 'Exercising my *droit de seigneur*, you mean?'

'What does that mean?'

'It means the medieval right of the lord of the estate to take the virginity of whosoever he chose. Except that there's no evidence that such a right ever existed.' He paused. 'And you were no virgin.'

The words hung in the air like undetonated bombs—and yet didn't it come as something of a relief to be able to explode them at last? 'Neither were you, Titus,' responded Roxy quietly. 'Though, let me guess—you're one of those hypocritical people who believe it's advantageous for a man to have had loads of lovers, but that there's something uniquely tacky about a woman who chooses to do the same.'

'I would describe it less as hypocritical and more of a biological imperative,' he drawled. 'Nature programmed men to go out and spread their seed as much as possible in order to ensure survival of the species.'

'Oh, please don't give me that old line,' she scoffed. 'If we were still operating according to those outdated laws, then I'd be sitting in some cave wearing a piece of animal skin and you'd be out clubbing some poor animal to death before breakfast. Though come to think of it—you *do* hunt, don't you, Titus? So maybe that much hasn't changed.'

He was smiling, even though her outrageous statement only reaffirmed her general unsuitability for rural living. But despite knowing that, part of him couldn't help but admire her feisty defiance because most women tended to lie or to play down their sexual experience. And wasn't that one of the things he had most liked about her—her honesty and her straight talking?

'I think you'd look rather good wearing a piece of animal skin,' he murmured as he brought the car to a halt. 'And if you could just stop talking for a moment and look over there, you'll see the sea.'

Following the direction of his gaze, Roxy turned to see a coastline which was unfamiliar to her and that first glimpse of the wide, pale sands and the lacy froth of the water almost took her breath away. The flat landscape made the horizon look limitless and the huge sky gave off a spectacular light and suddenly she could understand why painters and writers had always gravitated to this part of the world.

'Oh, Titus—it's amazing!' she breathed as she scrambled down onto the hard sand.

He locked the car and they set off together, though he frowned when he discovered she had no gloves and warmed her frozen fingers between his palms before insisting she wear his own rather battered leather ones. He buried his bare hands deep in the pockets of his jacket as they strode along. But the wind was so strong—buffeting at her with the persistence of an overenthusiastic puppy—that she looped her arm in his and felt him squeeze his elbow against her, as if he approved. And Roxy's heart missed a beat. Wasn't it strange, she thought wistfully, how walking arm in arm along a windy beach could somehow feel just as intimate as lying naked in bed together?

They walked until the sun began to sink low into the pearly grey of the winter sky before setting off back towards the car.

'Would you like to go for tea in Burnham Market?' he asked. 'Reputedly the prettiest village in the whole of England. It's not exactly the season for afternoon tea, but I'll have a word with someone and see what they can do.'

'I'd…I'd love to,' said Roxy, feeling stupidly *shy*—because hadn't she thought that he'd brought her to the deserted beach because he didn't want to be seen with her?

The village was quiet and it wasn't difficult for Titus to commandeer a table by a roaring log fire, in the heart of a cute old pub. Whatever 'word' he'd had with the owner had obviously been a very effective one since before long a pot of steaming tea, scones and jam and a plate of delicious-looking cake was presented to them.

Titus poured tea and Roxy sat back in her chair and at that precise moment she felt more contented than she could ever remember feeling. And contentment had a seductive charm all of its own. The warm flicker of the fire spread over her flushed skin and she tingled from the effects of the fresh air and exercise. It felt so *right*, she thought—just being with him and feeling so at ease with herself. To watch the glint in his pewter eyes as their gazes locked in silent communication, and he smiled at her in a way which was making her feel positively *mushy*. Recklessly, she blocked out the warning bells which were beginning to ring inside her head and instead she feasted her eyes on the man opposite her.

Afterwards, he took her into a small and very old-fashioned women's clothing store and asked to see a selection of gloves.

'Certainly, Your Grace,' murmured the shop assistant. And if she wondered who the Duke's blonde companion was, her face didn't show it.

Roxy left the shop with her hands snug in pale mauve cashmere—not the most practical of colours, but she had loved them on sight. She flexed her warm fingers and shot him a glance. 'That was very sweet of you. Thank you.'

'They're just gloves, Roxanne,' he said repressively.

But to Roxy they felt like much more than that. They were a gift from the man whom she'd fallen in love with. They were a tangible reminder of this perfect afternoon—when an impossible dream had seemed almost within grasping distance. When they'd walked along a beach and she had allowed herself to start imagining a 'for-ever' moment which was never going to happen.

'They're actually very pretty gloves,' she said lightly. 'And I'm just minding my manners by thanking you.'

He smiled. 'Then you must forgive me for my rather boorish response.'

It was dark by the time he dropped her

off near her cottage and she turned to look at him, trying not to sound *too* eager.

'Aren't you coming in?' she asked. 'Amy's out tonight.'

His initial impulse was to hurry her inside and to ravish her, but Titus hesitated. This afternoon had left him feeling...*unsettled*. It had all been a little too *comfortable*. He liked to think of Roxy as his cherry-nippled, imaginative lover and not a woman whose cold hands he had warmed and then drunk a cup of companionable tea with.

'I'm think I might drive up to London,' he said.

'London?' Roxy's expression didn't alter. She wanted to demand why he was going to London and who he would be seeing there. But she had no right to ask him, she realised. No rights at all. She dredged up one of those smiles she always turned on when a member of the paparazzi used to spring out at her from behind the bushes. 'That's nice.'

'Mmm. There are a few things I need to do—but I'll be back in time for the party.'

'That should come as a relief to the guests,' she said drily.

His lips gave a flicker of a smile and he almost regretted his decision as she got out of the car and brushed a strand of dark-blonde hair from her eyes. But he told himself that this was something he needed to do. Distance was necessary when you started seeing danger signs ahead. Start sitting by log fires with a woman and the next thing you knew, she'd be organising your diary for you.

'I'll see you Saturday,' he said.

'Yes, you will.'

Roxy watched the tail lights of the car disappear and went into the cottage, where she sat down on the sofa and stared at her new gloves and a strange and terrible kind of certainty washed over her. She had tried to fight it but she could fight it no more. She loved him. She *loved* him. It was as simple and as complicated as that.

And it was hopeless. A hopeless, misdirected emotion for someone who would never consider loving her back. Why, today was the first and probably the last time she would ever be seen with him in public. He had an image to maintain and a title to protect and she was nothing but a temporary fixture in his privileged life.

She slept restlessly that night and in the morning she was unexpectedly summoned to see Vanessa. She felt a chilling whispering of fear as she walked into her office. Had someone reported seeing her out with the Duke? And was the rather terrifying housekeeper about to tell Roxy that she had behaved inappropriately and was no longer needed?

Vanessa was sitting behind an intimidatingly tidy desk, with not a hair out of place. She looked up when Roxy walked in and gave one of those enigmatic smiles she was so good at.

'Ah, Roxanne. Good. I wanted to talk to you about the Duke's party on Saturday.'

Roxy nodded. *Say the kind of thing you'd be expected to say.* 'Everything's going according to plan, I hope?'

'It is, but we're going to need some help with the pre-banquet drinks. You don't have a problem with doing some waitressing, do you?'

Roxy brushed an imaginary fleck of dust from her pink overall, certain that she'd caught a glint of amusement in the housekeeper's eyes. *She's* enjoying *this,* she thought to herself. *Does Vanessa suspect what's going on with me and Titus, and is doing this to remind me of my proper place here?* 'I've never done any waitressing work before,' she said truthfully.

Vanessa's smile grew determined. 'Oh, don't worry about that. We've employed professionals to serve the food—all you'll have to do is circulate with a tray of champagne before the banquet begins. I'm sure you won't find serving drinks to His Grace's guests too onerous a task, will you, Roxanne?'

Roxy managed not to wince. In normal circumstances, maybe not. She'd got used to cleaning people's houses, hadn't she? And that had been a humbling enough experience, especially after her heady, youthful brush with fame. But this was *different.* She'd been the Duke's lover for almost a month. She'd been hidden away for most of the time like a guilty secret and that she'd just about been able to tolerate. It was just that the thought of serving drinks to his guests and having them look through her as if she were some kind of nobody made her feel slightly sick.

But you are *a nobody,* she reminded herself painfully. *That's exactly what you are. You're the woman who polishes the floor of his drawing room or flicks her duster over the priceless books in the Long Library. Oh, you might make him moan in bed and thrill him with the occasional snatched kiss—but you're nobody special in his life and you never will be.*

It was something she'd known all along, but this order from Vanessa felt like having it shoved in her face. Titus's birthday party would demonstrate the reality of his life and it was a life which didn't include her. His glittering friends would bring him glittering gifts. They would laugh and joke about a shared past and look forward to a shared future. Inevitably, he would dance with lots of gorgeous women—and she'd be forced to watch, circulating in her waitress uniform with a glassy smile fixed to her face as she offered them drinks.

She wanted to ask Vanessa if Titus himself had okayed this request, but she didn't dare. She wondered if the housekeeper had waited until he was out of the house for a couple of days to drop this particular bombshell, until she told herself to get real. Did she really imagine that the Duke might have intervened on her behalf? Told the housekeeper who'd worked for him for years that he didn't want this particular cleaner serving his guests because she was special? Because if she thought that, then she needed her head examining.

'No, that'll be fine,' Roxy said, suddenly becoming aware that she needed to booster her lukewarm response. 'I'm more than happy to oblige.'

'Good,' said Vanessa, with a quick smile. 'And Amy will be there to help you, of course—so you won't be completely on your own.'

The news that Amy would be joining her made Roxy brighten slightly, and later that morning she was removing some dust from the pouting profile of a Greek god in the Statue Gallery when her housemate walked in, beaming from ear to ear.

'So I hear from the big, bad boss that we're both going to be floating round as waitresses on the big night.'

Roxy gave a last flick over the statue's tight, marble curls. 'It seems we are.'

'So why the long face?'

'I didn't realise I had a long face.'

'Well, you do. If it was any longer, I could throw a saddle over your back and lead you round the stable-yard.' Amy's expression grew thoughtful. 'I wonder, could it have anything to do with the fact that you're having some sort of *thing* with our honourable employer, the Duke?'

To Roxanne's dismay, her duster clattered to the ground and it sounded deafening in the vast and echoing space. She could feel the guilty racing of her heart as she looked at her housemate. 'What did you say?' she breathed.

'Well, you are—aren't you? Getting it on with the gorgeous Titus?'

Flushing, Roxy bent to pick up the duster, the brief distraction giving her a moment to try to compose herself. She liked Amy too much to tell an outright lie but how honest could she possibly be in the circumstances? She straightened up. 'How did you guess?' she asked.

'Oh, come *on*, Roxy!" Purposefully, Amy walked over to the double doors and shut them quietly before turning round again. 'You mean, apart from the fact that sometimes when I'm coming back from the pub I can see him striding away from the cottage? Or the fact that he can't seem to take his eyes off you whenever he's around? He watches you like one of those deer they stalk on one of his weekend house-parties.'

'He doesn't,' Roxy said, but the flare of hope in her heart was quickly extinguished by the crushing reality of her situation. Even if he *did* watch her, it was only because he was physically attracted to her. But that was as far as it was ever going to go.

'Yes, he does,' said Amy. 'He gets a look on his face which is positively *primitive*.

As if he'd like to haul you off to the nearest bedroom and throw you down on the bed. Ooh, it makes me go all weak at the knees just thinking about it!'

'Oh, Amy.'

'Oh, Amy—what? There's no need to look so tragic about it. I don't blame you for getting involved,' said Amy, warming to her subject now. 'I mean, what woman with a pulse would turn down the opportunity of a fling with him? He's absolutely gorgeous. The only trouble is that he—'

'Yes, I know. I know,' Roxy put in quickly. 'He's a Duke and I'm a commoner.'

'Well, yes.' There was a pause and when Amy next spoke, her voice was wary. 'But you're far too sensible to have gone and fallen in love with him, aren't you, Roxy?'

'I don't do love,' said Roxy quickly, parroting the answer to a question she'd been asked by journalists a million times before. But for the first time in her life, her words didn't ring true. She could see Amy watching her and she wondered if her momentary lapse in concentration had given away the fact that she was being economical with the truth. 'But I do like him,' she admitted cautiously.

'Liking can be dangerous, Roxy.'

'I know it can. But it's not going to be dangerous for much longer. I'm only working here up until his party,' Roxy said. 'Which means I'll be leaving soon. And I'm not...' She hesitated—wanting to say the words out loud. No, it was more than that. *Needing* to say the words out loud. As if saying them would make them feel real. Would make her start believing them. 'I'm not holding out any unrealistic thoughts about the future. I'm not that naive. I know better than anyone that life never turns out the way you want it to. I just wish I could give him something for his birthday, that's all. Something he'd really like. Something to remember me by.' Rather self-consciously, she shrugged. 'I know. It's a stupid idea.'

'No, it's not.' Amy's eyes narrowed. 'I think it's a brilliant idea.'

'In theory, maybe. But there's nothing I could possibly give him which wouldn't fade into insignificance next to all the ex-

pensive gifts he'll get from other people.
I can't possibly compete with that crowd.'

'Oh, I think you can.' Amy gave a slow
smile. 'You could give him something
which nobody else could—and I'm not
talking about your amazing body.'

Roxy frowned. 'Then what *are* you talking about?'

'He's gone away for a couple of days,
hasn't he? Which gives you just the opportunity you need to prepare a very special
birthday present.'

'Which is?'

'What all the best presents should be.'
Amy grinned at her. 'A surprise.'

CHAPTER NINE

Valeo Hall had never looked more magnificent.

Adjusting his cufflinks so that the leonine Torchester crest gleamed against the whiteness of his dress shirt, Titus looked around the great hall. Initially, he had given his consent to this birthday party more out of duty than desire. He had agreed with the trustees that it should be a semi-formal declaration of his elevation to the Dukedom— but inside he had been quietly dreading it. The buzz of expectation and the sense of being assessed had filled him with a mixture of boredom and dread. Yet now that the evening was finally here, he couldn't deny feeling a glow of pride and satisfaction as he gazed around his ancestral home.

The vast dimensions of the rooms, which

sometimes dwarfed smaller gatherings, always lent themselves superbly to parties such as these. The opulence of the décor meant that there was no need for any embellishment. No balloons or banners or party-poppers. He shuddered. Perish the thought! Just lots of fresh, cut flowers and tall, fat candles illuminating the many beautiful artefacts. The kitchens were producing a giant version of his favourite *Sachertorte* as a birthday cake and the finest vintages had been brought up from the Torchester cellars. A band had been hired and a pyrotechnician was currently setting up the fireworks, which would be lit soon after midnight.

There was only thing which was missing...

Titus frowned. He had spent a day longer in London than he had intended. He'd done it because it had seemed to make good sense. He had found plenty to do and he had wanted to shake off the pervasive hold which Roxanne Carmichael somehow seemed to have exerted over him. Because she seemed to have crept into his thoughts rather more than he had intended and that needed to stop.

He had approached this dilemma with ice-cool logic——comparing it to one of those practice exercises he used to do during army manoeuvres, at school. He'd reasoned that once he was back in London he would easily be able to put her from his mind. After all, he'd never had any trouble compartmentalising lovers in the past—particularly ones who'd had such a shadowy presence in his everyday life. But the unpalatable truth was that he'd missed her. He'd missed her supple body in bed and the tickle of her long hair brushing against his belly. He'd missed the irreverent little asides she sometimes came out with when they were in the middle of some vehement debate and which he suspected he wouldn't tolerate from anyone else but her.

He flexed his fingers, objectively observing the whitening of his knuckles as he cursed his inexplicable *obsession* with her. Maybe he just hadn't had enough of her yet. Maybe he just needed to…

'*Roxanne?*' His voice rose on a note of

surprise as he saw a familiar figure approaching, yet one whose appearance was slightly out of kilter.

'Good evening, Your Grace.'

'What the hell are you doing?'

Roxy glanced around, just in case Vanessa was on the prowl. She had been jittery all afternoon—terrified that the housekeeper would discover what she was intending to do. Time after time she thought of the audacious plan she'd concocted with Amy's aid and wondered if it was too late to get out of it. And now it all seemed like the craziest idea in the world, especially as Titus looked so toweringly *formal* in his dress suit, with his tawny hair gleaming beneath the cascading chandelier. He looked like a man who had the world at his fingertips—who wanted and needed for nothing. Was her birthday surprise going to look like some tacky gesture he would secretly be appalled by?

'What does it look like I'm doing?' she questioned brightly.

He frowned. 'Why are you dressed as a waitress?'

'Because tonight I *am* a waitress. And tonight, Your Grace—I will be serving you and your guests limitless glasses of the finest champagne the Torchester cellars can offer. Vanessa has asked me and Amy to help with the catering,' she explained, when she saw his frown deepen. 'And we're actually being paid double time to do it.'

Her flippant comment about payment made him wince but it served to remind him that at least she was being pragmatic, even if he wasn't. But how the hell could he be anything but lustful when she looked like one of those women who graced the pages of men's magazines? Like a fantasy come to life. Her slim figure was shown off to perfection by the little black dress and those black stockings were making her long legs look positively sinful. Titus fought against the seductive taste of desire as he contemplated dragging her behind the nearest ornate pillar to kiss her.

'And why wasn't I consulted about this?' he questioned testily.

'Are you usually consulted about staffing levels at parties?'

He glared at her, knowing that she had a point. Such a thought wouldn't even cross his mind under normal circumstances—and it would be highly inappropriate if he brought up the matter with Vanessa now. But it meant that he'd have to spend the evening watching Roxanne dressed up in that sexy outfit, serving his guests—and the thought of that disturbed him far more than it should have done.

The dull ache at his groin intensified as he stared at the soft curves of her unpainted lips and he knew he had to get away from her before he gave into temptation.

'I'll see you later,' he said.

Roxy licked her lips as his grey eyes seared into her. 'You'll be too busy with your guests.'

'No, I won't. I intend being very busy with you—so make sure you keep the bed warm.'

And with that, he walked away, leaving Roxy regretting her passive agreement to such a tryst. Wasn't it a little *cheap* to agree to a late-night visit when the party was over? For him to spend the evening dancing with all the posh girls, but then re-tire with his cleaner for a little more basic entertainment? And wasn't it a little risky, with Amy around?

But any misgivings about her lack of assertiveness were soon dissolved by the enormity of the action she was about to take. Roxy's nerves grew, along with a bubbling sense of excitement as the guests began to arrive. She was so preoccupied that she failed to be intimidated by the more stunning women who must have raided their family vaults, judging by the amount of precious finery they were wear-ing. Several times she met Amy's complicit smile as they handed out glass after glass of bubbly.

The only time she felt a twinge of some-thing approaching apprehension was when she caught Titus's eye across the crowded ballroom. When he glittered her a look which seemed to exclude everyone else in the room. She felt a corresponding wave of emotion sweep over her, a fierce longing which made her feel momentarily weak. Was he going to hate what she had in store for him? Would it taint his memory of her? She could feel her heart pounding heavily beneath her uniform dress—but she knew it was too late to back out now.

The three hundred plus guests were soon being seated for the formal banquet and Roxanne was officially supposed to be helping clear plates in the kitchen. She worked unobtrusively in the background and managed to slip away just before the dancing began, to check with the band-leader that he knew what to do. Her heart was beating like crazy as she scurried through the labyrinth passages of the servants' quarters to where Amy was waiting in the boot-room, to help her get ready.

She had never been quite so nervous when she'd finished changing into her outfit. Not even when The Lollipops had performed at Windsor Castle, one unforgettable New Year's Eve. Walking in the dress she'd chosen was a nightmare. It was so tight that she had to shuffle along, terrified she'd split it, and already the wig was making her head feel hot and itchy. With the white fur stole draped around her shoulders and Amy darting ahead to check that the coast was clear, Roxy slithered into the curtained area behind the specially erected stage and let the band know she was there.

After a couple of minutes, the music stopped and the sound of chatter filled the ballroom. Roxy's heart was pumping and she was filled with a familiar hit of adrenalin as she waited to go on. It seemed ages since she'd experienced the dimming of the lights and the amplified voice of the bandleader and she could hear the room quieten as he began to speak.

'Ladies and gentlemen,' he began. 'Some time near the middle of the last century, a President of the United States of America had a very beautiful young actress sing to him on his birthday. And tonight, I have someone who wants to do the same. So here, for one night only—I give you…Miss Marilyn Monroe!'

Titus's head jerked up as he saw the figure who had appeared in the spotlight, her dress so tight that she looked as if she'd been sewn into it. And it was such an iconic image that he recognised her immediately,

even though the actress had died years before he'd been born. He heard the collective
gasp of the guests as her eyes searched the
ballroom until she had located him, but he
was so mesmerised by her appearance that
it took a moment for her identity to sink in.
And then his eyes narrowed in disbelief as
he met her smoky gaze and realised just
who it was.

Roxanne!

She let the white fur stole slide away
from her shoulders to reveal a breathtaking
vision beneath. The tight, flesh-coloured
dress gave her curves where he'd never noticed curves before. And it was covered in
hundreds of sparkling rhinestones so that it
seemed as if she were wearing nothing but
body glitter. The blonde, candyfloss wig
and the red, shimmering lips made her look
uncannily like the actress and as she picked
up the microphone and breathlessly began
to sing her eyes didn't leave his face.

'Happy birthday to you.

Happy birthday to you.

Happy birthday...' her voice dipped even
lower and she fluttered the outrageous

black arcs of lashes which were feathering her eyes '...*Duke of Torchester.*

Happy Birthday to you.'

Titus stood perfectly still as the audience erupted with rapturous applause and he thought that was the end of it. But no. She had held up her hand for silence and suddenly he caught a glimpse of the woman she had once been. The one who could command the attention of thousands of people by the sheer power of her stage presence. How she must miss all that, he thought. She'd gone from mass adulation as a pop star to cleaning other people's houses—without any apparent sullenness or resentment at the hand which fate had dealt her. *Yet was it really appropriate for her to have turned his birthday party into some sort of showcase for her own talent?*

The crowd grew quiet as she began to speak, her husky American accent mimicking the late film star perfectly.

'A lot of people don't realise that a second song was sung for the President that night and, because it seems somehow appropriate, I'm going to perform it tonight for the Duke. So, Your Grace—this one's especially for you.' She glimmered him a smile. 'I hope you like it.'

Titus stayed unmoving as she began to sing 'Thanks for the Memory' and as the first strains of the old, familiar song filtered out it made the little hairs stand up on the back of his neck. He watched the shimmering sway of her body and the scarlet gleam of her lips. And he knew what she was doing. She was saying goodbye to him in her own very distinctive way. He felt the strange kick of his heart as her voice—strong with passion and husky with regret—curved smokily around the lyrics. He felt the lust he was no doubt intended to feel—the hard jerk of an erection at his groin. Yet an undeniable part of him was slightly appalled that a private message from her to him was being made so very publicly.

And then it was all over. The spotlight was cut and when the lights went up again, the stage was empty and there was a roar as the guests started clapping and whooping their appreciation.

People were surging towards him, their faces full of curiosity, and Titus knew that he had to find her. *To say what?* Ignoring anyone who tried to halt his progress, he walked with grim determination through the ballroom and people fell back to let him pass. Where would she be? he wondered. She must have got changed somewhere in the house because no way could she have tottered all the way from her cottage in that dress and those heels.

Outside the ballroom he saw a waitress he vaguely recognised who was looking at him with big eyes and an expression which looked a little like guilt. 'Amy?' he questioned uncertainly, because wasn't this Roxanne's housemate?

'Yes, Your Grace,' she said.

'Do you know where Roxanne is?'

There was a pause as Amy bit her lip.

'Because if you do, I'd like you to take me to her right now,' he said, his tone leaving her under no illusion that she would be in big trouble if she didn't.

'Of…of course, Your Grace. She's…in the boot-room down by the kitchen.'

Titus nodded and pulled open the green baize door which led to the servants' quarters just as he heard the sound of running footsteps behind him. Turning round, he saw a breathless ex-schoolfriend, his face bright red with excitement as he skidded to a halt.

'For God's sake, Titus—that was the sexiest thing I've ever seen! Who the hell *is* she?'

Titus opened his mouth to reply, his mind racing as much as his thundering heart. He was aware of Amy looking at him. Of the sensation of being cornered. Of the look of pure lust in the man's eyes.

'She's nobody,' he said harshly.

CHAPTER TEN

ROXY heard him. He must have opened the heavy green door which had been designed so that no intrusive sounds from the servants' quarters would ever penetrate the hallowed portals of the big house. Which meant that his words rang out and reached her—like a verbal assault to her ears.

'She's nobody.'

The harshness of his assessment made her momentarily stumble and all she could think of was how *unfair* life could be. Couldn't he at least have *pretended*? All that time and trouble to give him a birthday surprise—thinking she was giving him something which might make him smile—and he could ruin it all with two cruel words. Roxy scratched at her itchy forehead as she tottered towards the boot-room.

But he was only giving voice to something she'd suspected all along, wasn't he? And could she really blame him? If you let a man *treat* you like a nobody, then you could hardly act outraged when he admitted it to the rest of the world. She had leapt into this ill-judged affair without a second thought. The first touch of his lips had been enough to make her forget about her ambition and her hopes for the future. From being a jobbing cleaner who had worked to fuel her dreams to sing, she had become the furtive consort of her aristocratic employer. Like some kind of joke figure from the Victorian era, she had turned into a below-stairs lover, with no real status of her own.

She could hear footsteps behind her and she resumed her unsteady pace, but it was a long time since she'd worn shoes this high and the dress was so tight that she couldn't run. The servants' corridors were like a warren—but as she heard his steps growing closer it didn't surprise her that Titus must know them like the back of his hand.

She made it to the boot-room and yanked off the wig—pulling all the tight clips from her hair so that she could scratch her fingers through her unbearably itchy scalp.

And that was the moment he walked in, slightly out of breath—his grey eyes unfathomable as they met her gaze. For a moment they just stared at one another.

'That was some birthday present,' he said slowly.

Her mind was working overtime. She didn't know how to play this. How best to get out of his life with the minimum of hurt and aggravation. Or was that asking for the impossible? Some lingering shred of professional vanity made her lift her chin to ask, 'Did you…did you like it?'

'Did I like it?' He gave a short laugh. 'I'm not sure that it was entirely appropriate, but it blew me away. Or, rather, *you* blew me away. You were sensational, Roxanne.'

'I'm glad,' she said, but inside she could feel a sinking sense of disappointment. *Appropriate?* Couldn't he forget his damned status for more than a minute?

Titus let his gaze drift over her. Without the wig, her head now looked like Roxanne

Carmichael but her body was pure Marilyn
Monroe and he felt the sudden rush of desire which made him want to throw caution
to the wind. Wouldn't it be best to brazen
this out? To take her back into the ballroom
and enjoy her beauty and her talent and to
hell with the consequences? 'Would you
like to come back to the party, and dance
with me?'

The unexpected question caught Roxy
completely off-guard. She touched her
messy hair, which was spilling untidily
over her shoulders, completely at odds with
the sleek, glittery gown. 'You mean, like
this?'

'Any way you want,' he said. 'I can always wait for you to brush your hair out
or put your wig back on. I don't care. I just
want to dance with you.'

For a moment, Roxy was tempted by a
scenario she'd never thought could happen. She imagined going back in there as
his partner. Imagined the thrill of being
led onto the dance floor and taken into his
arms. Because even though she sensed that
part of him disapproved of her over-the-top

gesture, she knew he was proud of her performance. She'd given him the ultimate in original birthday presents and now, in that very alpha way of his, he wanted to show her off.

For a moment she allowed herself to go along with the fantasy. She could picture the jealous faces of all the women who had been seeking his attention all evening. She could imagine the hard warmth of his body as they moved in time to the music. It would be very clear to everyone that they were lovers and she wouldn't have been human if she hadn't wanted that. But what would be the *point*? Wouldn't it only give her a taste of a life which could never be hers, no matter how many impromptu cabarets she organised in his honour? All she would be was a very shiny trophy on his arm.

'Roxanne?'

His question broke into her troubled thoughts and as he pulled her into his arms she knew she had to give him an answer. She'd been so caught up in the fantasy that she'd forgotten one vital thing.

She was a nobody.

Playing for time, she tilted her chin up and he leaned forward to kiss her throat. 'I can't face going back in there among all those people,' she said. 'Or having to answer a million questions. I'll just head back to the cottage. It's going to be a long night here. I'll see you tomorrow, Titus.' But she knew that by the time he awoke she would be long gone.

Titus felt the thrust of her breasts through the sheer material of her dress and he closed his eyes as his body tensed with a desire so intense it felt almost like pain. 'Or you could spend the night here,' he suggested unsteadily.

For a moment, she thought she must have misheard him. 'Excuse me?'

'Here. Or, more specifically—in my ducal bedchamber,' he said, his grey eyes glittering with humour as he deliberately used the outdated description.

Roxy wanted to laugh and yet she *didn't* want to laugh. How dared he try to make her laugh when this was no laughing matter? When she'd never been good enough to take to his bedroom before and she *still* wasn't good enough, not really. She shook her head. 'I don't think so.'

His fingers tightened around her arms. 'For God's sake, Roxanne—isn't that what you wanted all along? Why the hell not?'

Roxy flinched. He made it sound as if her only intention had been to try to worm her way into his bed. 'It isn't important,' she muttered.

'Well, actually, it is. It's important to me. I want you here with me tonight. In my house and in my bed.' His voice lowered into a silken whisper. 'And don't you realise that I always get what I want?'

She realised only one thing at that moment and that was how two-faced he could be. This wasn't some grand gesture of letting her know how important she was to him. He wanted her in his bed like some ego-feeding prize—while a few minutes ago he had just dismissed her to one of the guests as if she were worthless. She had been a shining star tonight and this was to be her reward. Restricted access had tem-

porarily been lifted and Roxy Carmichael
was being allowed into the ducal bed!

For a moment, she considered telling
him just what he could do with his offer.
That she knew *exactly* where she stood and
maybe it was time she bid farewell to all
her romantic dreams. But this sensible op-
tion was quickly superseded by another
very emotional one. Because even while
her heart rebelled at what he'd said about
her—her body still ached for him as much
as it had ever done. She wanted Titus Alexander and she loved him. So why *shouldn't*
she have one last night with him—a night
that neither of them would ever forget?

'Okay,' she said, forcing all the dark
doubts from her mind as she picked up the
carrier bag containing her jeans, sweater
and sheepskin boots. 'I will.'

'You certainly know how to keep a man
on tenterhooks,' he commented drily.

Roxy forced a smile. 'I know where your
bedroom *is*, of course—but perhaps you'd
better take me up there yourself. I'd hate to
run into Vanessa along the way. Then you

can go back to your party and I'll wait for you there.'

Titus shook his head. 'But I'm not going anywhere. There's only one party I'm interested in right now—and that's the one which is going to take place in my bedroom.'

Roxy told herself that his corny words meant nothing but that didn't stop her traitorous body from softening in response to them. He caught hold of her hand and she let him lead her through a set of corridors she'd never been in before and which turned out to be a short cut to his bedroom.

In normal circumstances she might have been intimidated by the thought of spending the night in the canopied four-poster bed, which looked impossibly large and grand. But what *were* normal circumstances? Roxy didn't think she'd ever known what most people thought of as normality, though maybe everyone felt like that, deep down. You were always measuring your life against other people's experiences—and your own always seemed to fall short.

Titus had shut the door and was now slipping the white fur stole from her shoulders. 'How the hell did you manage to pull this off?'

Roxy forced a weak smile. If things had been different, she might have told this particular story with laughing recall—but now it just felt like an episode she'd rather forget.

'There's a dress-hire place in London,' she said. 'Someone I knew from my days in The Lollipops.'

'Well, you look…amazing.' Deliberately, he let the tip of his tongue slide against the parchment dryness of his lips. 'Now come here before I die with frustration.'

Mindlessly, she went into his arms and let him kiss her. *I'm going to miss this,* she thought as she opened her mouth beneath his. *I'm going to miss this so much.* And wouldn't you know it? That tonight he was kissing her with a passion which took her breath away, or maybe it was all made more profound by the significance of being in his stately home. It made what was about to happen seem unbearably poignant and she knew that she needed to slow the pace down. Pushing her hands against the hard muscle of his shoulders, she took a step back. 'I'd…I'd better take this dress off.'

'Here, let me.'

'It's very delicate.'

'I think you'll find that I can be gentle, Roxanne,' he murmured.

She wanted to cry because she realised that he could. Very gentle. His fingertips were whispering so softly over her body that her heart felt as if it were about to shatter with hopeless longing.

He peeled the dress away from her body and made a barely audible sound as he stared at her. 'You're…' He swallowed. 'You're not wearing anything underneath.'

'I couldn't—not even a thong, I'm afraid. It's a very unforgiving dress.'

'Roxanne—' He said her name in a way he'd never said it before as he hung the dress on a chair and pulled her into his arms.

For one brief moment she wanted to ask why he had ruined everything—why he had denounced her in such a cruel way—

but she was so fired up by desire that she began to undress him with a fervour which was equal to his.

He was laughing as she tugged the clothes from his body until they were both completely naked. Or at least, *he* was. Roxanne was still wearing the towering gold stilettos which put her eyes almost on a level with his. As if she'd read his thoughts, she bent to slide them off.

'Don't,' he said roughly. 'Leave them on.'

But Roxy shook her head as she ignored him and took them off anyway. She was through with playing any more parts. She wasn't going to conveniently morph from Marilyn Monroe into his stereotype of a perfect lover—naked but for her glittery gold shoes. Tonight she wasn't going to be anyone but herself—the essential woman beneath all the different layers which had been constructed over time and by circumstance.

'Kiss me,' she said.

He heard the slight break in her voice and it spoke to something deep inside him as he carried her onto the bed, laying her down on the velvet crimson cover so that she looked like a medieval painting. He felt the bed dip beneath his weight as he joined her and began to kiss her, his mouth moving from her lips down to the cherry-tipped nipples. She writhed as she felt his tongue licking against her belly and she tugged at his shoulders, urging him back up—so that his face was looking down into hers.

'No. Not like that. Not this time,' she whispered.

He nodded, slipping on a condom he suddenly had no desire to wear before slowly entering her. Instantly, he lost himself in her tight heat and as she wrapped her legs around his bare back it felt as if she'd suddenly taken lack of inhibition to a whole new level. Because this was Roxanne on fire. Her kisses were deep and drugging. Her hands seemed to whisper over every inch of his skin—working an exquisite magic wherever they touched. He heard himself gasping with helpless pleasure as she took control.

She was whispering things into his ear. Things he could barely make out through his heightened senses. He felt the tension building. He felt as if his body was going to explode—as if he might die with desire for her. She gave a wild cry as she orgasmed around him and his own responding cry sounded guttural as his seed pumped deep inside her.

Afterwards, he felt curiously shaken— even more so when he felt the wetness of her tears against his face. His normal response would have been to put distance between them—because women and tears were never a good combination, especially in bed. But Titus was as contented as a jungle predator who had just been fed a large lump of juicy flesh, so instead he lazily turned his head and traced a thoughtful finger along the smooth damp surface of her cheek.

'Roxanne?' he said, but she didn't answer and his question was forgotten as fireworks began to erupt in the sky outside the huge windows of his bedroom. He shook her gently by the shoulder. 'Someone must have given the order to light them. Look out there.'

Obediently, Roxanne stared straight ahead, trying to concentrate on the lavish display as she watched the fireworks explode in the night sky. Silver. Gold. Pink and blue. There were sunbursts and cascades—their whirring sounds mostly drowned by the accompanying strains of classical music. Fireworks to celebrate the birthday of the eleventh Duke of Torchester, with no expenses spared.

'They're wonderful,' she said, dredging up what passed for enthusiasm from some dark and empty place deep inside her.

'Aren't they?' He bent his head and brushed his lips over hers. 'And perfect timing, don't you think?'

'Oh, perfect,' she echoed, but her heart felt as if it were breaking and she had no one to blame but herself. She had signed up for this. The nobody who had made the mistake of thinking she was somebody. She had walked right into an affair which had never been intended to last, thinking that she was strong enough to cope and it turned out that she wasn't. The warmth of her orgasm was fading into a terrible iciness which was encasing her body as she lay perfectly still.

Comfortably Titus snaked his arm around her waist, hooking her closer so that her bare bottom pushed against the already hardening thrust of his groin. Later, he thought lazily. He would make love to her later. And he let his heavy eyelids drift down to a close.

Roxanne lay in his arms for what seemed like hours, listening to the sound of his deepening breathing until she was certain he was asleep. Gingerly, she shifted an exploratory leg to the edge of the bed and although he stirred slightly—he did not waken.

Her movements were silent as she picked up the golden shoes and put them carefully in the bag, along with the rhinestone dress and the white fur stole. Then she slipped into her jeans, sweater and sheepskin boots and let herself out of Titus's room.

She needed to be careful. The party was still going on and if she ran into Vanessa at this point it would be little short of nightmare. Like a shadow, she slipped from the house and ran over to her cottage just as dawn was breaking. It was one of those incredible winter mornings with nature providing her very own firework display. Pale apricot and coral light blotted out the fading stars and the great house looked very beautiful against the lightening sky.

She wondered what Titus would do when he woke. Would he wonder where she had gone—or simply be relieved that she had slipped away without fuss?

She was shivering by the time she let herself into the cottage and quietly crept up to her room. Gathering together her things, she began to lay them on the bed. Packing was one of the things she was really good at—but then, she'd had enough practice when she was touring. Efficiently, she layered her clothing in the suitcase—and was just wondering whether she could hitch a ride to London from one of the party guests when she heard the front door open.

She knew it was Titus, but presumably he wasn't calling out for fear of waking Amy. She found herself praying that he might just turn around and go out again if she didn't go downstairs to greet him.

Her breathing sounded unnaturally loud as she heard the sound of his footsteps on the stairs. And then suddenly, he was standing in the doorway of her bedroom looking dark and powerful and more than a little intimidating.

For a moment he said nothing—just looked from her face to the suitcase and then back up to her face again.

'Going somewhere?' he questioned.

She wanted to scream. To fling herself at him with a burst of heartbroken tears— but Roxy knew that a scene would only complicate things. It would make leaving even more difficult and she needed to stay calm. To show him that she'd thought this through. Most importantly of all—to let him know that she wasn't going to change her mind.

'Well, that *is* what is usually implied by someone putting clothes in a suitcase.' She raised her eyebrows at him in mocking question. 'I thought you'd know that better than anyone.'

'You're leaving?'

She heard the incredulous note in his voice and part of her had to admire his incredible chutzpah. 'Yes, I'm leaving. It was never intended that I should stay after your party.'

'Maybe it wasn't. But isn't this just a little dramatic? Slipping away from my bed in the middle of the night, without bothering to tell me?'

'You were asleep.'

'Please don't insult my intelligence, Roxanne. You could have woken me up.'

She wedged a shoe down the side of the bulging case. 'Maybe I was saving us both the embarrassment of bumping into one of your guests—or one of the other staff.'

'Surely that's something for *my* consideration, not yours?'

His arrogance made something inside her snap and Roxy straightened up, all her good intentions to stay calm deserting her. 'You just can't help yourself, can you?' she accused. 'You make this big, *magnanimous* gesture about letting me spend the night in your precious bedroom—yet you still can't help yourself from acting superior! I thought I was there last night as your equal—'

'And you were!'

'Well, if that was the case—then I'll decide when I leave. I don't need your permission, Titus.'

His face darkened with frustration. He was not given to voicing his emotions, nor to analysing them. Over the years he had learnt to observe other people's behaviour but never to react to it. But suddenly he found himself breaking one of his own rules. 'I thought that your timing was particularly bad, in view of what had just happened.'

'You mean, because we'd just had sex?'

'Do you have to put it quite so crudely?'

She shook her head, determined not to be sucked into any more fantasising, but it wasn't easy—not when it was your heart's dearest desire. 'But why wouldn't I be crude, Titus—when I'm nothing but a *nobody*?' She saw him flinch. Saw the growing comprehension in his eyes as he made the connection and she geared herself up for the showdown she'd been hoping to avoid. 'Beginning to get the picture now? Because I *heard* you! I *heard* you telling that man that I was nobody!'

He frowned as he recalled his throwaway comment to his old schoolfriend and his mouth hardened. 'I did it because—'

'No!' she flared back, seeing his dark expression as she cut through his protestation. 'I don't want to hear your pathetic excuses! There's no possible explanation which would make that ever seem all right!'

'You don't think so?' he questioned, a slow anger beginning to simmer away inside him. 'Then forgive me if I fail to be impressed at your lack of perception. I actually did it to protect you.'

She gave a slightly hysterical laugh. 'To protect me?'

'That's right. Because I didn't want you having to contend with any speculation—or questions. The kind of questions you once told me you hated. I thought that exposure as my lover would open you up to all that picking over of your past.'

'Or future?' she said quietly, because

she didn't believe him. She didn't want to believe him—because if she thought that he'd acted out of kindness, then wouldn't it make walking away impossible? 'Your future.'

'My future?'

'Yes, of course. You were protecting yourself, Titus—and maybe I don't blame you. Because if the world found out that the Duke of Torchester had been sleeping with his cleaner—then wouldn't that prompt the kind of questions which *you* wouldn't want to answer?'

His voice was silky. 'Questions such as what, Roxanne?'

'A story like this would be a gift for the tabloids,' she said. 'Put two high-profile people together and suddenly the world starts speculating about marriage.'

He gave a bitter laugh as his gaze raked over her, because now he was on very familiar territory indeed. 'I think that you're forgetting that you are no longer high profile. And it sounds to me like *you're* the one who's been speculating about marriage, sweetheart.'

His words rang out with cruel aristocratic clarity and something inside Roxanne seemed to shrink and die as she saw
the imperious look on his face. He was
doing it again, she realised. He was pulling rank—telling her that he was important
and she wasn't. He just couldn't help himself—that was his default mechanism. No
matter what she said or did, she was just
some little woman who couldn't wait to get
her hooks into him. Well, he was wrong if
he thought she could ever tolerate life with
such an arrogant tyrant as him.

'I think you flatter yourself, Titus—if
you really think I've been plotting how to
get you up the aisle.' She paused, wondering just how big she could make the lie.
Whether she could bring herself to say
something so fabricated that it would bring
the whole affair to a conclusive end. 'As far
as I was concerned, it meant nothing at all
to me. It was just a fling, that's all.'

'Nothing?' he repeated incredulously, because women didn't do this to him. *He* was
the one who did the leaving.

'That's right. And a very enjoyable fling,

I must say. We've both had them before and we both know when they've run their course—which this one most definitely has. So I'm going. Vanessa's got my bank details—if you could make sure that the money I'm owed goes in my account, I'd appreciate it.' She sucked in an unsteady breath. 'I'm not sure whether you count what happened between us last night as overtime, but—'

'Oh, for God's sake, Roxanne!' he bit out furiously. 'Will you *stop* this?'

'I've stopped.' She held up her hand for silence, the way she'd done at the party just a few short hours ago—only this time she had an audience of just one. 'There's nothing more to say and I'd like to go back to London as quickly as possible.'

His heart was pounding heavily in his chest, as if he'd just been running a race. 'If you walk out of that door—then it really *is* over,' he said harshly. 'Do you understand?'

'Yes, Titus.' Meeting his eyes with a defiance she wasn't sure she could hold onto for much longer, she gave a short laugh. 'I understand perfectly.'

CHAPTER ELEVEN

THE London house seemed unusually quiet—and unusually cold—as Titus let himself in. Maybe the heat of the Kenyan sun was responsible for the chill he felt on his skin as he put his passport and bags down in the hallway. Or maybe it was something to do with the fact that last time he'd been here, it had been with Roxanne. When he'd been in control and *felt* in control as he'd fed her antibiotics and glasses of water. When he'd thought he was doing her a favour by taking her up to Norfolk and offering her a damned job.

What he hadn't anticipated—nor ever could have anticipated—was that she would leave behind a memory which was proving infuriatingly difficult to shift. Even a complete break in the baking African heat didn't seem to have made a dent in it. He marched into the drawing room, poured himself three fingers of whisky and took a large mouthful.

Damn her!

The day after his party—when she had followed through with her dramatic threat to leave—he had booked himself on an impromptu safari trip to Kenya. He had figured that some winter sun was just what he needed to forget her. That and the undeniable thrill of watching nature from a close but safe distance. It had been a while since he'd visited Africa and the country was as beautiful as he remembered. He'd thrown himself into an exhausting round of activity. He'd ridden horses—and camels. He'd fished, he'd walked and he'd eaten beneath the stars. And, politely but very firmly, he had rebuffed the advances of a beautiful American heiress who was staying in the same camp.

What else could he have done when Roxanne's face was continuing to haunt him—appearing in his fractured dreams with alarming regularity? Sometimes he would waken, his body screaming with tension as he wondered whether the threat of some natural predator outside his tent had caused his senses to be so instantly alert. But no. The only threat was the turbulent nature of his thoughts and a sense of impatience that he couldn't manage to rid himself of her seductive memory.

He walked over to the phone to see that the message box was completely full and he yawned. They could wait. He would take a long shower followed by a good night's sleep and tomorrow he would tackle the work which had built up in his absence. He wanted to prolong his vacation by one more evening—because hadn't one of the best things about it been the complete lack of modern amenities? No phone. No computer. No TV. Life was certainly simpler without the constant interruptions of modern life.

But habit made him switch on his mobile phone to see that it was also full of messages from numbers that he didn't recognise. It started ringing immediately and he saw that it was Guy Chambers, who had

treated Roxanne when she'd had pneumonia. Could Guy also wait until tomorrow?

Maybe not. He sighed, knowing that he
couldn't keep the world at bay for ever. He
clicked the connection. 'Hello?'

'Titus?'

'Funnily enough, I do usually answer my
own phone.'

'Where the hell have you been?'

'I took a safari trip to Kenya. A kind
of late birthday present to myself.' Titus
frowned. 'Why, should I have checked with
you first?'

There was a brief silence. 'Have the press
been in touch with you?'

'No. Why would they?'

'So you haven't seen the Net?'

'No, thank God. I'm happy to say that I
haven't been near a computer for an entire
fortnight.'

'I think perhaps you should.' Guy's voice
sounded more than a little strained. 'Try
typing "Marilyn + Duke's totty" into You-
Tube and see what happens.'

Titus froze. 'What the hell's going on, Guy?'

'I think you should ask Roxanne,' said

the medic. 'It seems that maybe she's trying to resurrect her career on the back of her association with you.'

With an angry little snarl, Titus cut the connection and went immediately to his study, staring out of the window as the computer fired into life, barely noticing that the winter drabness had been broken by the monochrome splash of the snowdrops which carpeted the oak tree.

His mouth was dry as he tapped in the bizarre key words, until a rectangle appeared on the screen with the frozen image of Roxanne at its centre. He pressed on the arrow and the image began to move—all blonde hair and scarlet lips and that incredible glittering body looking almost as if it were naked as she sang. He heard the husky and very sexual inflection as her voice lingered on the words *Duke of Torchester*. With a growing feeling of nausea he watched the clip all the way through, registering that it had received over a million and a half hits. And then he clicked onto the search engine and typed in the words *Roxy Car-*

michael + *The Lollipops*—and it all began to make sense.

There were thousands of items about Roxy singing at his party. There was speculation that they were lovers—confirmed by an unnamed guest at the party claiming to have seen the two of them disappearing into Titus's bedroom. But most damning of all was the news that The Lollipops' *Sweetest Hits* had shot up the charts and that there was now a very real possibility that the group would re-form.

Titus was so angry that he slammed his fist down on the sycamore surface of the desk, only just missing the inlaid Sèvres porcelain which had made his acquisition of this rare piece so difficult.

How dared she?

How *dared* she?

He wanted to blaze round and confront her, until he realised with a start that he had no idea where she lived or even where her father lived. That Roxanne Carmichael lived an itinerant life, which only reinforced her general unsuitability to be anything other than a member of his staff.

But the gypsy-like quality of her existence made him momentarily pause as he tried to get his head around the instability of her lifestyle. What must that be like? he wondered. To have known such fabulous wealth until the crackpot investments of her father had left her with nothing. No money and no real place to call home. Until he forced himself to remember how ruthlessly she had exploited their relationship and his anger made him pick up the phone.

After speaking to someone at his club, he quickly hired a private investigator and by the following afternoon he had the information he needed. She had a live-in job, working as a chambermaid at the Granchester Hotel. Her hours were from six until midday and then she spent a further two hours, between four and six, turning down the guests' beds for the night. Her room (537) could be found on the fifth floor of an anonymous-looking block at the back of the hotel complex.

It almost killed him but he forced himself to wait until she had finished work, damping down his natural inclination to storm round there and demand that she be removed from her shift and brought to see him immediately. That was what he would have done in the past, he realised. Been unable to wait. Used his status to have the rules bent for him. So what had changed?

In the grey and drizzly early evening, he drove to the back of the hotel and, shortly after six, saw a familiar figure appear through a side door and make her way through the car park. She was wearing some kind of hat, the brim shielding her strained features, and she hugged her jacket close to what looked like an alarmingly slender frame. He felt his heart leap in his chest but he sucked in a deep breath until he had composed himself, reminding himself that she had used him as ruthlessly as any woman could use a man.

He gave her ten minutes while he listened to the news—the stories of bombs and rebellion not really registering as the minute hand ticked slowly around his watch. And then he locked his car and made his way over to the tower-block, riding up in the utilitarian grey metal lift to the fifth floor.

His thumb paused over the doorbell of number 537 and he realised that a jumble of feelings was making him feel…*angry*. No, it was more than anger. It was uncertainty, too. What if she wasn't alone? What if that pale and supple body was currently writhing underneath *another* man? Viciously, he jammed his finger hard on the bell and then had to wait so long for an answer that he began to wonder whether the investigator had got the right apartment.

And then she opened the door and Titus found that just seeing her again made his first snarled accusation die on his lips. And he couldn't for the life of him work out why. She'd lost weight again. Far too much weight. And her eyes were looking at him with an expression he couldn't make out. Was it guilt? he wondered grimly.

So why was his heart beating with all the frantic irregularity of a man who had just been confronted by a goddess? Yes, she wore a dress and a pair of boots, which emphasised her amazing legs. But it was a very *ordinary* dress. Nothing special. What *was* it about her which made him seem to lose a grip on his sanity whenever she was in the vicinity?

Her tongue was sliding over the surface of her bare lips as if she was summoning up the courage to say something and he thought he had never seen her face look so pale and so bleached.

'What are you doing here, Titus?'

He walked straight past her, his eyes rapidly searching the boxlike accommodation of bedroom and bathroom until he walked into a drab sitting room—relieved to find it empty. But his trembling rage remained.

'I've come for some sort of explanation.'

'I beg your pardon?'

'Please don't insult my intelligence by feigning ignorance, Roxanne. We both know why I'm here. Surely there must have been part of you which had been expecting this?'

Slowly, she nodded, because, yes, she had. Only she'd thought that he might come looking for her sooner—ready to spill out the rage which she could see was contorting his aristocratic features. Yet his anger now seemed almost inconsequential because all she could think was how infuriatingly *alive* he looked—this most vibrant and powerful of men. His skin was deeply tanned and it made his brilliant grey eyes gleam like moonstones. The aching in her heart came back, stabbing painfully beneath her breast. He must have been away, she thought as she registered the healthy glow of his skin—which was probably why this inevitable confrontation hadn't happened sooner. But seeing him again was far worse than she had ever imagined it would be. It brought back memories of what it had been like to lie in his arms. It made her recall the time when he'd bought her those beautiful mauve gloves. The times she'd stroked her fingers through his tawny-thick mane of hair. She shivered, knowing that she needed to get rid of him. Before she did something stupid—like begging him to make love to her just one more time…

She cleared her throat. 'You're talking about the video clip?'

'Yes, I'm talking about the video clip! The video clip which seems to have been seen by half the world!'

'Or by one and a half million inhabitants of the world to be more precise,' she corrected tiredly.

'Don't try and get smart with me,' he said furiously. 'Just tell me when you decided to do it. Was it before or after you slept with me? I guess it must have been afterwards—because the story wouldn't have had legs if we hadn't been lovers.' *Lovers*. The word seemed to ring round the room and mock him. As if there had been anything like love involved in what had happened between them, when all the time she had clearly been using him as collateral. Safeguarding her future with a gem of an idea—a publicity coup to end all publicity coups.

'Is that what you really think?' she questioned woodenly.

'It's not a question of what I *think*, Roxanne—it's a question of what I *know*. You gave a very fine and sexually loaded performance in front of a lot of very influential people and you got someone to film it.'

'But I didn't know it was being filmed!' She met the disbelieving elevation of his eyebrows and suddenly she couldn't bear him thinking that she could cold-blood-edly exploit him like that. 'I borrowed the costume from someone I'd known in my Lollipop days—because I could never have afforded to hire something like that. They had it couriered down from London and when they found out what the address was, they realised…'

Her words tailed off with embarrass-ment and Titus iced a disgusted stare at her. 'What did they realise, Roxanne?'

She swallowed. 'That you lived there. And that this could be a perfect market-ing opportunity. So they hid in the house and when I came on to sing, they…they filmed it.'

Titus nodded. 'So not only have you made me a laughing stock,' he said, in a cold and deadly voice, 'but you're telling me that you also posed a security risk by letting some stranger into my house?'

Roxy shook her head. This was worse than she'd ever imagined. She had been prepared for his fury—she had almost *wanted* it. Because hadn't her own rage almost equalled his? When she had discovered what they'd done *she* had felt exploited, exposed and picked over—as if a colony of vultures had stripped her bare. But she could see from the iciness of his grey eyes that it would be a waste of her time to try to convince him of that. Titus believed what he wanted to believe. What he'd always believed. That she was a low-end kind of person—deserving of sex, yes, but not of the consideration he might show to a woman of his own class. Otherwise, wouldn't he have listened to *her* side of the story instead of first condemning her?

'What do you want me to say?' she questioned tiredly.

'I want you to admit that you used me.'

There was a moment of silence as her indignation struggled to break free. *Used* him? Why, she had *loved* him. Loved him as she'd loved no other man, nor ever thought she could. Loved him even though she'd struggled not to—until her feelings had won out over common sense. The injustice of it all began to bubble up inside her until she told herself that maybe it was easier this way. If he went away from here believing that she was a taker, then he would never come back. Because the alternative would be to convince him of her innocence and then what?

They would kiss and make up. They would have passionate sex—probably right here in this institutional little apartment. And once the gilt of all that exciting make-up stuff had worn off, reality would set in. There was no possible future for them—there never had been and there never would be. Titus would look for a way to escape and she would be left nursing a heart even more wounded than it felt at this moment.

But if he stormed out of here, convinced of her duplicity…

'Yes,' she said woodenly. 'I used you. I used your ducal status and high-profile party for publicity purposes. It was an opportunity too good to resist. Are you satisfied now, Titus? You've had my confession in full and you can just shut the box on all your memories of me and pretend that I never existed. But if you don't mind, I'd rather you did it elsewhere. I'm going out.'

From the swirl of his confused thoughts, he felt as if he were in the midst of some unspeakably bad dream as he took in her long legs and the knee-high boots.

'Is it a man?' he questioned sourly.

She drew a deep breath. *You can do this, Roxy. You can convince him you're the woman he thinks you are.* 'I'm afraid it is,' she said quietly.

Titus flinched as a wholly unexpected stab of pain dwarfed even the fierce crushing of his ego. For a moment pride urged him to haul her into his arms and to kiss her and then demand to know whether any other man would ever make her feel the way that he did. Would ever make her moan with pleasure, the way that he did.

But wasn't that an arrogant thing for him to think? Was it really so inconceivable that for the first time in his life he had met a woman who didn't consider herself lucky to be on his arm? A woman who had decided that he had behaved unfairly towards her during their liaison? Maybe she'd met a man who wasn't keeping her hidden away because of the vast social gulf which existed between them. Maybe it had been his own behaviour towards her which had made her decide to exploit him.

He felt a twisting sensation in his gut. He wanted to say sorry but something stopped him and he couldn't quite decide whether that was because it was too late, or because saying sorry had never come easily. So instead, he nodded. Shrugged his shoulders as if to acknowledge that the best man had probably won. It was the most exemplary display of cool good manners he'd ever exhibited and, wryly, he thought that his mother would be proud of him.

'Then I must wish you every success in your future, Roxanne,' he said, before turning on his heel and walking out without a backward glance.

He barely registered his journey down in the lift and realised he was shaking by the time he reached the car. A fine mist of rain clung to his tanned skin but he didn't bother wiping it off. It was almost as if he *wanted* the wet chill of the winter day to sink deep into every cell of his body. He debated whether to drive home,

or to his club—but a restlessness and in-
ability to focus made him change his mind
and walk instead into the main foyer of the
Granchester and then into the Piano Bar.

He guessed he could get very drunk and
order a taxi home later on, but instead he
sat in the shadows at the back of the bar,
staring morosely at his untouched glass
of whisky. He hadn't been here in a long
while, not since Ciro D'Angelo had owned
it—and thrown some of the best parties in
the city. Sometimes Titus used to fly over
from Paris to join the great and the good
who used to congregate here.

The room was dominated by a rather
starry white piano and the deep blue of
the velvet wall hangings gave the illusion
that the room was high up in the night sky.
A middle-aged man in a dark dinner suit
had come into the bar and sat down at the
piano, his fingers breaking into a medley of
songs from popular musicals. And wasn't
life full of irony at times? thought Titus
bitterly. Because the third tune he played
was the poignantly familiar 'Thanks for the
Memory'. It was a song which a beautiful

but doomed actress had once sung to her equally doomed President. A song which Roxanne Carmichael had sung to him.

And he had thrown it back in her face.

He lifted his glass to take a first sip of whisky, when it suddenly hit him like a punch to the solar plexus—and he wondered why he hadn't thought of it before. Putting his glass down, he lifted his hand to his forehead and rubbed it, as if doing that would make him see clearly. But he wasn't seeing clearly at all. His thoughts were so dazzled by the foxy woman he'd just left that somehow he had overlooked the fatal flaw in his logic.

Because if Roxanne had used him to publicise herself and her band—if she was planning to resurrect her career on the back of it—*then why the hell was she working as a chambermaid?*

Suddenly, none of it made sense and all of it made sense. Did she look like a woman who was poised on the edge of a musical comeback? Did she?

Had he been, at best, stupid? Or at worst—cruel?

A shaft of pain shot through him as he saw how quick he had been to judge. How quick to wield the knife and to send accusations hurtling her way.

His hands were shaking as he pulled out his wallet and, peeling off a note, he put it down on the table next to his drink. He felt as unsteady as if he'd drunk a bottle, instead of a single sip and he wanted to go straight across the rainy car park to that anonymous block. To ride up in the lift and tell her...tell her...

He walked out of the bar, impervious to the smile of the brunette who was sitting at the bar and who raised her glass of champagne at him in a hopeful toast.

Tell her what? What could he possibly say which would ever make Roxanne forgive him for what he had said, and done?

CHAPTER TWELVE

Roxy stifled a huge yawn as she brought the trolley to a halt outside the heavily embossed double doors leading into the Maraban suite. She was tired. No. Scrub that. She was *exhausted*. Worn down by lack of sleep and by the unfamiliarity of starting to read textbooks again. And, of course, she was worn down by the overwhelming heartbreak of missing Titus.

She felt a renewed wave of misery wash over her. That was easily the most debilitating cause of her fatigue. Unsociable hours she could cope with and hopefully the art of studying would soon return. But the pain which twisted so relentlessly inside her—would that ever leave her?

Swallowing down another yawn, she pulled the master key from the pocket of her apron. Already that evening she had serviced twenty rooms, carefully turning the sheets back and plumping up the pillows so that they were as soft as clouds. Being a chambermaid had been a new direction for her and had certainly given her a few insights into human nature. People often left their rooms looking like pigsties, she had discovered. Or maybe they were just proud of their sexual activities. It didn't matter how classy the hotel—and the Granchester was certainly classy—some guests seemed to have no qualms about leaving discarded bits of underwear scrunched up in among the rumpled sheets. One morning she'd even found a used condom!

Still, she only had one more bed to turn down and then she could escape to the peace of her little room and try to do some reading. Try to do anything, really—as long as it didn't involve lying on the bed, nursing her heart and thinking about the man who had broken it.

She thought back to yesterday evening when Titus had turned up out of the blue— looking all tanned and vibrant and making her feel insubstantial just by being close to him again. She thought about the rage which had contorted his face as he'd hurled those bitter accusations at her—and the way she had just stood there and let him. Why had she done that? Swallowed her pride and been so passive in front of him? *Because that was the best thing to do,* she told herself fiercely. *The only way you could guarantee he would leave you alone.*

Picking up two chocolates from the trolley, she gave a polite rap on the door of the suite. She'd left this one until last, mainly because it was her favourite, named after the homeland of one of the hotel's most famous guests—an exotic sheikh who had once stayed there.

She had just stepped into the gold-and-rose coloured interior when she saw a figure sitting at the desk in one of the windows with his back to her—and her heart gave a jolt. Her fingers curled nervously around the foil-covered chocolates she was holding. 'I'm so sorry, sir. I thought the room was empty. I did knock, but…'

But the words died on her lips. The blood

began to roar in her ears because the figure was getting to his feet and turning round. A figure with a powerful physique and hair the colour of burnt copper. The blood drained from her face as she met the pewter gleam of his eyes. For this was the stuff that dreams were made of. Or nightmares.

'What...what are you doing here?' she questioned shakily.

Titus stood completely still as he surveyed the pallor of her face and the haunted expression on it. She looked so vulnerable, he thought. There was a terrible sadness in her blue eyes, which were very bright, as if she'd been crying. Had he made her cry? *Had* he?

'I'm staying here,' he said.

Roxy shook her head, angry with him now. 'I gathered that. But why? You've got a house in London.'

For a moment he was overcome by a wave of remorse so bleak that he felt it wash over him like a dark and bitter tide. 'Because I wanted to speak to you on neutral territory.'

'Why? I don't think we've got anything left to say to each other, Titus.'

'Oh, I think we do. Or at least, *I* do.' He sucked in a hot and unsteady breath. 'I've come to say sorry.'

Roxy swallowed down the prick of tears—determined that he wouldn't see her cry. Hadn't she cried enough tears over him already—stupid, salt tears which had soaked her pillow night after night? 'Sorry won't cut it, I'm afraid,' she said.

Titus met the look of stubborn fury on her face and felt his heart twist. Had he thought this would be straightforward? That a few words of apology would have her flying into his arms and covering his face with grateful kisses? He tensed. Perhaps he had.

'I don't blame you for being angry with me, Roxanne.'

'That's very generous of you.'

Slowly, he nodded, acknowledging her sarcasm as nothing more than his due. 'I should have known that you'd never do something as cheap as exploiting our relationship to further your career.'

'And when did you manage to work that out?' she questioned tiredly.

'When I realised that you wouldn't be doing a job like this if you'd relaunched your career.'

She nodded. 'But you couldn't just take my word for it, could you?'

He met the challenge in her eyes and it felt like having a sabre plunged deep into his chest. 'No,' he said harshly. 'It seemed I couldn't. I was a fool—and so I say to you again that I'm sorry. And believe me when I tell you that I will never misbelieve you again.'

She shook her head, steeling herself against the look of contrition which had darkened his steely eyes. He thought it was all so *easy*, didn't he? Because it was. Everything always *had* been easy for Titus. Oh, maybe not his growing-up years, but certainly where women were concerned. He called the shots—and they let him. 'You're making it sound as if we have some kind of future together, Titus,' she said. 'And we don't.'

'But we could.'

'No!' Her word rang out with a bell-like clarity and she knew that she had to be brave enough to tell him. Because unless he understood that she meant this, then he might not give up. She knew that Titus hadn't finished with her yet—that the sexual attraction which had always burned between them was still sizzling away. And that if she wasn't careful, then their affair could be picked up and resumed. Could drag on for months—and where would *that* leave her when it finished once and for all? Feeling a million times worse than she did right now, that was where. But if she told him the truth then she wouldn't see him for dust.

'No, we couldn't,' she continued. 'Like I said, we don't have any kind of future together. End of story.'

His eyes narrowed. 'Why not?'

She stared at him, knowing that she had to be strong enough to admit her weakness. That she had to swallow her pride and tell him. She had to let him know that this wildly flamboyant gesture of hiring out the most expensive suite in the hotel—presumably so that he could drag her over to that enormous bed—didn't actually *mean* anything. It was nothing to do with the real, emotional stuff—it was all about sexual gratification. And it was no longer enough. 'Because I love you, Titus,' she said quietly. 'Because somewhere along the way—and even though I vowed it would never happen—I've fallen madly in love with you.'

'Roxanne—'

'No!' she interrupted—the words bubbling up in her throat in their eagerness to be spoken. 'Let me finish. I've fallen in love with you—but that happens to people all the time and they get over it. *I'll* get over it. But what I will not get over is if we drag it out—every exquisite moment a step closer to the inevitable end. Because I know it can never be more than a casual fling to you. I know you'll need to go hunting around for a suitable wife to give you the heir you require and you probably ought to do that sooner rather than later. I understand all that—I just don't want to be an understudy for the role any more, that's all.'

Titus felt his heart race as he listened to

her passionate outburst. He realised how much courage it must have taken for her to admit to loving him, when he had never given her any indication that his feelings for her went beyond the simply carnal. He had taken and taken from her and never given anything back and now it looked as if he was about to reap the bitter consequences of such behaviour. Never before had he felt as if a situation was so delicately poised on the brink of triumph or disaster—as if she held his very happiness in the palm of her hand. So tell her, you fool. Reach out and tell her before it's too late.

'And I don't want you to be an understudy,' he said, his words sounding unsteady as he saw everything that he stood to lose. 'I want you to take the starring role in my life. Because I love you, Roxanne. I love you so very much.'

'No, you don't!' Roxy realised that she'd been gripping the chocolates so tightly that she'd squashed them and, furiously, she stuffed them into the pocket of her apron. 'You're just saying that because you want to have sex with me!'

'That is true. I most definitely want to have sex with you,' he said gravely. 'But I also want to marry you. I want you to be mine—legally, physically and emotionally.' He took a step towards her, his face tense. 'I've been so wrong, Roxanne. I always thought I'd be forced to marry out of a sense of duty and that was why I looked on the prospect of marriage in the way a man might regard the hovering blade of a guillotine. But marrying for love is something entirely different. The thought of it fills me with...joy. And a very primitive kind of anticipation. I want to make you my wife. Or my Duchess, to be more precise.'

'Stop it,' she whispered. 'Please will you stop it, Titus? Words are cheap. Anyone can say them and not mean them.'

'I know they can,' he said fiercely. 'Which is why I didn't come rushing straight round to tell you this last night. Why I forced myself to wait until today, even though the effort of doing that nearly killed me. But I had to wait until my bank was open.'

'Your *bank*?' she echoed in confusion,

because for one crazy moment she thought he was talking about her wages, which she happened to know had been paid in full.

'Yes. Or more specifically—the vaults in my bank.'

'You're not making any sense.'

'Aren't I? Then perhaps I'd better let my actions speak for me instead.' He put his hand into the pocket of his trousers and drew out a small, very old-looking leather box and opened it. He heard Roxanne make a disbelieving little gulp, which became a shocked gasp when he dropped to one knee in front of her and took her trembling hand in his. 'Roxanne Carmichael, I love you more than my uptight words can probably ever convey and if you would do me the honour of becoming my wife, then I would be the happiest man on the planet.' He looked up at her and suddenly his voice was catching in his throat and he could feel the prick of tears behind his eyes. 'Because I can't bear to think of a future which doesn't include you, my darling. My life has been so empty without you.'

Roxy was staring from his eyes to the

ring, and then back to his eyes again and her mouth kept opening and then closing.

'You're supposed to say something,' he prompted gently.

It wasn't the ring which swung it—though it was the most beautiful thing she'd ever clapped eyes on. And it certainly wasn't a very feminine satisfaction that she of all people should be subjected to this most traditional of proposals. No, it was the look of love blazing from his grey eyes which made Roxy's heart turn over. Which made her realise that there was only one answer she could possibly give.

'Yes,' she whispered shakily, her determination that he shouldn't see her cry now melting away as tears of joy began to slide down her cheeks. 'Yes, I'll marry you, Titus.'

He slid the ring on her finger and slowly kissed the palm of her hand, before standing up to pull her into his arms so that he could kiss her properly.

After that, it all became a little frantic and conversation was reduced to gasped little words and whispered pleas until, several hours later, she lay wrapped sleepily in his arms in the giant bed. Reflectively, he stroked her hair and felt her long sigh of contentment as her breath fanned against his chest.

'Just one thing puzzles me,' he said slowly. 'Well, two things, actually.'

'Spill.'

'If your greatest hits album is topping the charts in several countries, then why did you need to get a live-in job which didn't pay very much?'

Roxy lifted her head. 'You mean, why wasn't I going out to put a deposit on a fancy apartment?'

'Something like that.'

She drew a little circle around one of his nipples and enjoyed his instinctive intake of breath. 'I don't think people realise how long it takes for royalties to come in,' she said seriously. 'They don't just land in a massive heap on your doorstep overnight. But the royalties are irrelevant, because I didn't write the songs. Justina did—and so all the money will go to her.'

He lifted her distracting finger and raised

it to his lips. 'Then why didn't you want to re-form the band?' he questioned. 'When you could have gone back out there on tour and made yourself a fortune?'

Roxy was silent for a moment. She couldn't deny she hadn't been tempted by the possibility, until the reality of what it would be like had hit her. 'Because immediately it became like a circus,' she said quietly. 'All those reporters asking all those questions again. The sense that I was nothing but a *commodity*. Touring was hard enough when I was nineteen—but at nearly thirty, it would have been a nightmare. And it would have been going back—revisiting the past instead of trying to move into the future.' She was silent for a moment, because only a few hours ago her future had looked very different indeed. But it was important for her to acknowledge that she had planned to be proactive. That she had been making plans to move on and to live a useful life, with or without Titus.

'I planned to study,' she said, with a smile. 'I thought I might do something useful, like speech therapy. I thought I might put my gift for mimicry to good use.'

There was a moment of silence while he considered this. 'You might find the demands of being a Duchess and taking on a new career a little much—'

She placed her finger over his lips to silence him. 'I know that, my darling,' she whispered. 'Marriage to you, and hopefully motherhood—that's the only career I'm interested in now.'

He lifted her hand to look at the clutch of antique diamonds which was glittering on her finger. 'I love you, Roxanne Carmichael,' he said. 'You make me laugh and you challenge me. You satisfy me and tantalise me and I can't think of anyone else I could better describe as my equal, in every way that counts.' He grazed his lips over her fingertips and as he heard her exultant little giggle he frowned. 'You haven't changed your scent, have you?'

'No, why?'

'It's just that you definitely smell of chocolate.'

With a start, Roxy looked across the

room to where her apron was lying in a heap with the rest of her discarded clothes. And there, just above the distinctive embroidered 'G' of the hotel crest, was a dark and spreading stain of finest Belgian chocolate. She looked deep into her new fiancé's eyes and smiled.

'Um, I think you may have to fork out for a replacement uniform, Titus.'

EPILOGUE

Roxy would have liked a quiet wedding in the Valeo chapel, followed by an unconventional picnic on a stretch of their own Norfolk beach. But she knew that it didn't work like that. Not now. That as the new Duchess of Torchester, she would have to make certain sacrifices. That duty would often have to come before desire—but she knew it was a duty she would perform gladly, and with pride. Not that it seemed much of a sacrifice to marry Titus in the glorious space of Norwich Cathedral—with its Norman architecture and famously long nave.

Once the rather hysterical press coverage of their engagement had died down, there had been a lot of speculation about who would be on the guest list. Titus's stepmother had already given a 'tell-all' interview to one of the tabloid newspapers, cataloguing the new Duke's cruelty towards her. *Titus Left Me Homeless!* ran the rather pathetic headline in the *Daily View.* Which, as Titus pointed out to Roxy, was blatantly a lie, since he'd bought her a sturdy manor house in the heart of the Cotswolds as well as a mews house in London. But it was her comment about Roxy's unsuitability to be a Duchess which gave him the perfect reason not to invite his stepmother to help celebrate their nuptials.

And in complete contrast, Titus's mother had welcomed Roxy into the family with instant warmth. A tall, striking woman with dark copper hair, she took Roxy walking over the wild Scottish moors near her home one weekend, and thanked her for making her son so happy.

The wedding day dawned bright and sunny—a perfect example of English springtime at its most glorious, with hyacinths forming a fragrant white arch around the cathedral doors. The crowd of photographers who were waiting to see if the other two Lollipops would turn up had a field day when Roxy's father arrived. He was wearing a crumpled linen suit and a hairstyle which was much too long for his years—and he was clutching the hand of a woman who was two years younger than his daughter.

'And did that bother you?' Titus asked her, much later.

She shook her head as she began to unbutton his shirt and smiled. 'I can't change him,' she said thoughtfully. 'I just have to try to love him.'

'You're good at that,' he said softly.

'Am I?'

'Mmm.' He leaned forward, his lips grazing against the curve of her jaw. 'The best.'

But loving Titus was easy, Roxy reflected as he began to kiss her. The easiest thing she'd ever done. Because to her he was not a Duke with centuries of tradition behind him and riches which most people could only dream of.

He was her love. Her man. He was her very heart and soul.

* * * * *